R.K. Narayan was born in Madras and educated there and at Maharajah's College in Mysore. His first novel, *Swami and Friends* (1935) and its successor *The Bachelor of Arts* (1937) are both set in the enchanting fictional territory of Malgudi. Other 'Malgudi' novels are: *The Dark Room* (1938), *The English Teacher* (1945), *Mr Sampath* (1949), *The Financial Expert* (1952), *The Man-Eater of Malgudi* (1962), *The Vendor of Sweets* (1967), *The Painter of Signs* (1976), *A Tiger for Malgudi* (1983), *Talkative Man* (1986), and his most recent, *The World of Nagaraj*. Other novels include *Waiting for the Mahatma* (1955) and *The Guide* (1958)—which won the Sahitya Akademi Award.

In 1980 R.K. Narayan was awarded the A.C. Benson Medal by the Royal Society of Literature and was made an Honorary Member of the American Academy and Institute of Arts and Letters. In 1989 he was made a member of the Rajya Sabha. As well as five collections of short stories (*A Horse and Two Goats*, *An Astrologer's Day and Other Stories*, *Lawley Road*, *Malgudi Days* and *Grandmother's Tale*), he has published two travel books (*My Dateless Diary* and *The Emerald Route*), four collections of essays (*Next Sunday*, *Reluctant Guru*, *A Writer's Nightmare* and *A Story-teller's World*), translations of Indian epics and myths (*The Ramayana*, *The Mahabharata and Gods, Demons and Others*) and a memoir (*My Days*). *Malgudi Landscapes*, a selection from Narayan's best writings, is also available in Penguin Books. *A Town Called Malgudi: R.K. Narayan's Finest Fiction* is forthcoming in Viking.

The Emerald Route

R.K. Narayan

PENGUIN BOOKS

Penguin Books India (P) Ltd., 11 Community Centre, Panchsheel Park, New Delhi 110 017, India
Penguin Books Ltd., 80 Strand, London WC2R 0RL, UK
Penguin Group Inc., 375 Hudson Street, New York, NY 10014, USA
Penguin Books Australia Ltd., 250 Camberwell Road, Camberwell, Victoria 3124, Australia
Penguin Books Canada Ltd., 10 Alcorn Avenue, Suite 300, Toronto, Ontario, M4V 3B2, Canada
Penguin Books (NZ) Ltd., Cnr Rosedale & Airborne Roads, Albany, Auckland, New Zealand
Penguin Books (South Africa) (Pty) Ltd., 24 Sturdee Avenue, Rosebank 2196, South Africa

First published by the Director of Information and Publicity, Government of Karnataka 1977
Published by Penguin Books India 1999

Copyright © R.K. Narayan 1977

10 9 8 7 6 5 4 3

Typeset in *Galliard* by Digital Technologies and Printing Solutions, New Delhi
Printed at Chaman Offset Printers, New Delhi

Contents

Introduction

I am grateful to the Government of Karnataka for the generous manner in which they had arranged for my travel in Karnataka to gather impressions and material for this book. They left us totally free (that's myself and my brother Laxman) to write (and sketch) as we liked, without offering any hint or suggestion at any time. And that enabled me to select and record aspects of Karnataka which appealed most to my mind.

Karnataka has many facets: several mountains, forests, rivers, a great deal of history, major schemes for power generation, industrial and irrigational projects.

Karnataka has been the home of great personalities like Sankara, Ramanuja, Madhvacharya and Basaveswara. Jain mystics, composers and mystics like Purandara Dasa and others. Eminent warriors and kings have appeared on the stage of Karnataka, played their parts and vanished into the wings. Every worthwhile and significant personality seems to have had his birth in this part of the land or arrived at a significant moment of his career.

It is not practical to cover all parts of Karnataka in a book of this kind, nor every aspect of each place mentioned. One has necessarily to be selective considering the encyclopaedic nature of the theme. Some places have been described at length, others have only been touched upon through a fragment of history, a local belief, a relevant anecdote, or a description of a personality or scene, all of

1

which, to my mind, are like the parts of a jigsaw puzzle—pieced together they could produce, for my readers, not only a total picture of the Karnataka I saw, but also convey the quality and texture of its men and culture.

Preamble

The earliest mention of 'Karnataka' occurs in a poem learnt at school, a story concerning a cow and a tiger. The cow, while grazing in a forest, is accosted by the tiger, who is hungry. Realizing that its end is come, the cow musters courage and pleads for time to go home, feed its calf, and return. The tiger relents and lets it go. Punctually, as promised, the cow reappears, ready to appease the hunger of the tiger, which is so moved by the honesty of the cow, that it jumps off a crag to its death.

After this poem, one looked on the cow as a creature of unquestioned integrity, and the tiger as a not-too-unreasonable creature, surprisingly sensitive. Apart from these reactions, the poem conjured up a picture of *Karnataka Desa,* the centre of the world (*Dharani Mandala Madhya*), as a land of forests, mountains, green pastures, cows and tigers. However, there was no hint of a sea coast in this or any other description, since the coastal areas had not yet become a part of Mysore State which consisted only of eight districts: Mysore, Mandya, Bangalore, Kolar, Tumkur, Chitradurga, Hassan and Shimoga. Kannadigas outside this orbit were scattered in the adjoining provinces—Bombay, Hyderabad, Madras and Coorg. After every battle, which was chronic, boundaries were shifted according to a victor's demands and fancy, and the population in the border areas pushed, pulled, and moved hither and thither. Kannadigas, more than any other linguistic group in India, suffered much this

5

way. They found themselves now under rulers who spoke Kannada, next under rulers who spoke Tamil, Telugu, Malayalam, Urdu, Portuguese, or English, no settlement lasting beyond one generation or two. In British days, the division of states was based on the administrative or strategic notions of an Imperial power. When the concept of Independence took root, Mahatma Gandhi and Jawaharlal Nehru advocated reorganization of the states on linguistic basis. The present Karnataka came into being in 1956. When all the Kannada-speaking areas were marked off and added to the old Mysore State, it turned out to be one of the largest single territories in India, with nineteen districts and a total area of 1,91,756,07 square kilometers.

THE LANGUAGE

Kannada is one of the four main languages of south India, of Dravidian origin, and the eighth among the languages listed in the Constitution. The earliest Kannada inscription is of the fourth century AD. A work of the ninth century, Kavirajmarga, quotes thirty-six earlier Kannada poets, and also mentions that Kannada was the language of the people from Kaveri to Godavari.

Apart from Sanskrit, Jain religion and literature influenced Kannada writing. Among the Jain writers, Pampa (942 AD) is well known. His *Bharata* and *Adipurana* are immortal works, known widely, read and enjoyed even today by literates and illiterates alike, the latter, perhaps, by the ear. Ponna (950 AD) wrote the story of Rama in fourteen chapters, Chavundaraya (978) stories of the sixty-three great Jain saints. Ranna's *Gada Yuddha*

(993) is being studied in the classroom even today. Stories and romances abound. Nemichandra wrote in 1170 a romance entitled *Lilavathi*, in which lovers meet for the first time in each other's dreams and then search out and marry after overcoming several obstacles in their path. Rajaditya (1191) wrote a treatise on mathematics. Many technical and scientific works were also written between the twelfth and fourteenth centuries on Ayurveda, poisons and antidotes, treatment of cattle diseases, on meteorological topics (entirely in verse) dealing with rainfall, cloud-formation, earthquakes, and underground water, thunder and lightning. In the twelfth century, after the fall of (the later) Chalukyas, Kallachuris became dominant in Karnataka. Buddhism, Jainism and Vedic religions were losing their dynamism; at this juncture, Basaveswara appeared on the scene with his *Vachanas*, terse and powerful epigrams, touching many aspects of philosophy and conduct, which created a new religious order; Kumara Vyasa (1400) has left an outstanding work in his *Bharata*. The musical compositions of the Dasas, Purandara Dasa, Kanaka Dasa and many others, wandering minstrels mainly singing the glory of God, are timeless in their appeal. The most popular at this time (as even today) are the *Tripadis* of Sarvajna. Sarvajna's exact date is uncertain (about 1700). He adopted a life of wandering with a begging bowl in hand. His two thousand verses in *Tripadi* meter express a pragmatic philosophy aimed at the common man, attacking hypocrisy, bigotry, and superstition, and some are also reflective or lyrical. *Tripadi* is a verse form in three lines, suited to folk music, lullabies or for the expression of one's longings and aspirations. The rhythm of *Tripadi* has an impact, which is immediate, universal and abiding. The

poet's words sank deep into the minds and hearts of people. It was indeed 'mass communication' at its best, achieved through the sheer potency of thought and expression, without any mechanical aids or talk of the 'Media'.

With the eighteenth century, Kannada literature entered the modern period (and continuing today), with its numerous poets, novelists and dramatists who carried on the influence of the earlier traditions, mingled with the influence of Western literature, and who have managed to leave behind what may safely be termed 'Great Writing', both in quantity and quality.

HISTORY

Karnataka has a complex history, not easily presented as a narrative progression in a 'horizontal manner'. Many strands of history have gone into the making of the present Karnataka complex. Several kingdoms flourished in the North, South, East and West, and rose and fell rather steeply, intermingling or clashing while they existed. When we speak of Karnataka history, we have to take into consideration the fortunes of several dynasties that existed at different times, and analyse the common features, which have contributed to the development of Karnataka.

A future scholar reviewing our present-day culture and the historical pattern is likely to conclude: '20th century history was made by inexhaustible speakers. All over the world, it was the same; the aspirant to a political throne had to utter several million words in his career, through all media, and hold on until a greater talker gained the ear of the public and talked him out of the scene.' History was made rather differently in earlier times. If we are to believe what our historians tell us, no ruler ever tolerated the idea of a fellow-ruler anywhere, but always strode the earth like a mighty colossus, with sword drawn, until he encountered his match, who would continue from where the other left off, until *he* found *his* match again. This was history and an endless process carried on by militant characters in the story, whatever name they went by, Gangas, Kadambas, Rashtrakutas, Hoysalas or Chalukyas.

Before history comes the legendary background. Every place in Kamataka has an association with an episode or a character in the Ramayana or the Mahabharata. Wherever you turn, you will find a legendary touch. For instance, at Chunchinakatte in Mysore, the river has a yellow tinge because Sita bathed in it. In Bhagamandala, in the Coorg district, the Pandavas used to be seen. In Tumkur, an eternal spring issues from a rock, which had been touched by Rama. The associations are widely placed. Dandakaranya, where Agastya dwelt, is identified in Karnataka. Tungabhadra, flowing near Hampi was the River Pampa of Ramayana. Vatapi of the epic is Badami in Bijapur district. When Parasurama had gifted away the entire earth and had no space to stand on, he appealed to the ocean king who rolled back and created the present-day Konkana.

Mahabharata mentions Karnataka in a listing of countries. And by about the third century BC historical associations begin. Chandragupta Maurya spent his last days at Sravanabelagola (96 km from Mysore) on Chandrabetta, having prepared himself to end his life in the Jain manner. The hill on which he spent his last days is known as Chandrabetta and faces the famous colossus

Gomateswara standing on the hill top across. Asoka's edicts inscribed on stone pillars are to be found in Chitradurga and Raichur districts. Satavahanas succeeded to the Mauryan empire in the first century BC. By about the fourth century, Gangas and Kadambas had become prominent powers, in north and south respectively. By about the sixth century the Chalukyas of Badami became powerful (535-757 AD). Pulikesi II (610-642 AD), grandson of Pulikesi the founder of Chalukyan line, subdued the Gangas among others and established his supremacy until in his turn swept off by the Pallavas. Rashtrakutas reigned supreme for two centuries from 753 AD, with their capital at Malkhed in Gulbarga district. Among the Rashtrakuta kings must be mentioned Amoghavarsha (refreshing to think of him in this welter of sword and fire), a unique ruler, who preferred peace to war, studies to conquests. He wrote *Kavirajmarga*, the earliest Kannada work on poetics, under the pen name of Nripatunga, and supported men of letters. Rashtrakutas were overthrown by Taila II, hitherto fairly obscure but a descendent of the Chalukyas. Ranna was a court poet in Taila's reign.

Vikramanka or Vikramaditya (1076 to 1126) was practically the last ruler in the Chalukyan line. He was so successful in war that he promulgated an era in his name in place of all other calenders. His exploits are well recorded in a poem by Bilhana.

During the twelfth century, the Chalukyan power declined and the Yadavas of Devagiri and the Hoysalas became prominent. The Hoysalas, who had their capital at Dorasamudra, rose to importance under Vishnuvardhana who died in 1141 after reigning for thirty years. His grandson Viraballala extended the dominion northward and clashed with the Yadavas of Devagiri (who were descendents of the feudatory chiefs under the late Chalukyas, and had become independent after the decline of the Chalukyan power). Viraballala's exploits made the Hoysalas the most powerful force at the close of the twelfth century and the capital Dwarasamudra—Dorasamudra or Halebid—was finally destroyed by Malik Kafur, general of Allaudin Khilji of Delhi, in 1326 or 1327.

Hakka and Bukka were the founders of the glorious Vijayanagar Empire with its capital at Hampi in 1336. This was also the period which saw the founding of Bahamani kingdom at Gulbarga. Ultimately the conflict between the Muslim rulers and the Hindu empire Vijayanagar, was the chief cause of the collapse of Vijayanagar rule by about 1565. The Bahamani kingdom collapsed in due course. Adil Shahi dynasty established itself in Bijapur in 1489, and ended in 1687, in the reign of Aurangazeb, who personally conducted a relentless campaign for the subjugation of the recalcitrant Muslim rulers of this area. After the fall of Vijayanagar, North Karnataka passed, successively, under the Muslims, the Maharattas, and lastly the British.

After Vijayanagar, power passed on to the Wodeyars of Mysore, and the chieftains of Keladi who ruled from Shimoga, the most famous among them being Sivappa Nayak, who gave succour to the last of the Vijayanagar kings, Sriranga Raya. Keladi lost its independence in 1763 when Haidar Ali invaded their country. Raja Wodeyar was the first of the Wodeyars (1578—1612), who had captured Srirangapatna, and was functioning as the Viceroy of Vijayanagar. In 1731 Dalavoy Nanjaraja seized power, and held on until Haidar Ali overthrew him. After Haidar Ali, Tippu became the ruler, and when he died in the Fourth

Mysore War, the British restored the Wodeyar line to a child of five years under the regency of Dewan Purnaiya. In 1831 the British took over the administration and restored it in 1881 to Chamaraja Wodeyar whose successor was the famous Krishnaraja Wodeyar the Fourth, who could be called the maker of modern Mysore.

We have necessarily to take a bird's-eye view of history, and skip at this point many names and dynasties and centuries. This is only in the nature of a survey to familiarize my readers with the general background of the Karnataka history.

Part One

The Emerald Route

The term occurred to me when we starred out on the first phase of a tour of Karnataka, from Mysore, through Hunsur and Hassan, and returned to Mysore nearly one week later, having continuously journeyed up and down the ghats. Konkan coast and Coorg, and never seeing a dry patch anywhere. Green of several shades we saw, mountain-sides lightly coated with verdure and fern, the dark foliage of trees rising hundreds of feet from the valley, light green, dark green, pale green, evergreen, and every kind of green shade, were offered for our delectation all through our circular tour of approximately a thousand kilometers.

The road to Hassan passes through rice fields on both sides, across the course of both Kaveri and Hemavathi rivers. This is the most unwearisome part of the journey by car since there is so much to watch—tiled farmhouses, or little shrines, or mantaps set amidst transluscent, waving paddy fields, and the roadside villages consisting of no more than a dozen houses along the highway, and displaying signboards of tailor shops, restaurants and hair-cutting saloons and hoardings advocating two-children families on all their walls. I used to live in Hassan over half a century ago, long before the railway was laid, when we had to reach it by bullock cart from Arsikere—an all-night caravan journey to cover twenty-seven miles. Hassan had only one main road, flanked by lantana hedges, and the homes of the district officials were set far back, beyond a drive of murmuring casuarina trees. My father's official residence, for a Headmaster, was a colonial style house with a trellised porch, covered with purple flowers, and guarded by a huge Gold Mohur tree, set in a three acre ground, amidst grass fields, where cobras also lived but at peace with us.

Now on arrival, I searched for this landmark. I was advised that our old house was now a hospital behind the Taluk Office signboard. Brick compound walls having replaced the lantana hedges, it was difficult to identify places. I could not locate our old house. Although the town is much changed today with new buildings and shops, and a Town Square, from where the roads radiate, its inherent charm (which for some reason I cannot understand made people name it 'Poor Man's Ooty') is still there. Its grassy downs, vista, and stately trees on the roadside are still there. From our window at the motel built amidst evergreen trees, we noticed thousands of bats hanging topsy-turvy from their high branches and squealing and squeaking. Banyan, Gold Mohur, and Casuarina are still there in abundance; the town has not grown at the expense of its tree population.

Hassan, apart from its own charms, is a portal through which one could pass into an ancient culture at the temples in Belur and Halebid. Belur, 32 km from Hassan, on the Yagachi river, is a small town; at a turning beyond a row of shops, one suddenly faces a temple, which is unprepossessing at first sight; but passing in, one finds oneself entering a paved corridor so wide and spacious that a whole town's population could be accommodated in it comfortably.

The Hoysala ruler, Bittiga had come under the influence of Ramanujacharya (whom he had sheltered from his Chola persecutors) and changed his name to Vishnuvardhana, marched against the Cholas, captured their capital at Talkad in 1116, and built a number of temples to commemorate his victory, the foremost among them being the one at Belur.

It was designed by Jakanachari, although, on the walls appear signatures of other sculptors such as Dasoja of Belgaum, Chavana, Nagoga of Gadag, Masana of Lakkundi, etc. Here we have the finest example of what has come to be known as the Hoysala style. The actual temple is mounted on a star-shaped basement, which you climb by a short flight of steps. All around the base are carved 650 elephant figures, each one in a different pose. On the rows above you find a variety of themes depicted. Ramayana and the Mahabharata and all the legendary characters or episodes are represented in minute detail, on every available inch of space, from bottom to top. Every nook and corner and angle is filled with figures and decorations. Moving along the circumference of the star-shaped pedestal, if you could spare about ten hours a day for examining each section of the wall methodically day by day, you could complete the viewing of the figures in fifteen days. The profusion seems superhuman. If you are in a group, you will be distracted by the excited calls: 'Come here, and see this; here is a marvellous composition of Vishnu's ten *Avatars*, as Vamana, Varaha, Narasimha, Rama, Krishna and so on. Nothing like it anywhere. Come for a minute, please.'

'Tell me, is this not Arjuna rescuing Virata's cows?' You may hear another exclaim, 'Did you notice the dancer at this angle? You must not miss this. Note the folds of her drapery!' At the same moment the seasoned guide will be flourishing his baton while explaining: 'You note that jack fruit, the fly settling on it, and the wall lizard poised to attack the fly.' You will be looking up and down all the time in consonance with the motion of his baton; he doesn't pause for breath while explaining; he doesn't even look at what he is pointing, being familiar with every inch of the wall. 'The lady is distressed while that monkey is tugging at her sari . . . Notice the overcoat on this figure with buttons, which proves that there were buttons in those days . . . This woman has done up her hair in pony-tail fashion, which is again popular today . . .' His jokes are seasoned to appeal to the tourists who come in waves all day long.

Inside the temple, the elaborate amount of work done on the inner wall of the central dome is to be seen by flood-light. (Formerly, they were illuminated by a mirror reflecting the sunlight.) The pillars in the hall are smooth, glass-like with polish, and lathe-turned, displaying a variety of designs. In the sanctum sanctorum, you see the seven-foot figure of Chennakesava, to whom all this artistry is dedicated, a god who imparts grace and protection when you watch Him by the lamp-light in the inner shrine.

HALEBID

Halebid is about 17 km east of Belur. Now a little town, with a population of less than 4000, although in its days of glory, it was the capital of the Hoysala kingdom and known as Dorasamudra. It is impossible to connect this picture with what one could conjure up as it must have been in

Hoysala times, a resplendent capital, teeming with life and activity, and crowded with visitors and plenipotentiaries from lands far and near. A little hillock named Benne Gudda, on the east, weed-covered, with a scrap of wall standing, is pointed out to us as the site of the palace. The historical cause for its ruin was the attack by Malik Kafur, Allaudin Khilji's general, who invaded the Hoysala dominion in 1310. The capital was completely sacked. There was some effort by the survivor Narasimha to rebuild it, after transferring his capital to Belur. In 1326 Mohamed Bin Tuglak sent another expedition and razed the city to the ground, leaving no vestige of the capital—except the street of potters, which has a legendary explanation. The extinction of Halebid or Dorasamudra was due to the curse of a woman. The king's sister had come on a visit to the capital, bringing with her, her two sons, who were handsome. One of the king's wives attempted to seduce the young men, and was repulsed. Enraged by her failure, she reported to the king that the boys had tried to molest her. The king immediately ordered his nephews to be impaled and their bodies to be exposed at the city gates. The mother, that is the king's sister, was cast out and the citizens were forbidden to give her shelter. She wandered the streets maddened by all this injustice, cursing her brother and his kingdom. She was given help and admitted only in the Potter's Street, and that is all that is left of the capital today, the only remnant of a grand empire. Although the human habitations of those times have disappeared, the temples built by Vishnubardhana and his successor stand to attest once more to the grandeur of the Hoysala reign and their artists. Hoysaleswara and Kedareswara temples attract crowds of visitors every day, from every part of the country and the world. The sculptures are more minute and intricate than at Belur, the architectural patterns remaining more or less the same, the difference being that the outer walls built on the terrace are worked out in greater profusion and detail than at Belur, while the sanctum of the temple is comparatively simpler. If, as I have mentioned, one needs ten hours a day to study and absorb the details of the work at Belur, double that time will be required to study the walls and their friezes here in Halebid.

Fergusson says of the Kedareswara temple: '. . . From the basement to the summit, it was covered with sculptures of the very best class of Indian art . . .'; of the Hoysaleswara temple: 'It's perhaps the building on which the advocate of Hindu architecture would like to take his stand. Unfortunately, it was never finished, the works having been stopped after they had been in progress for eighty-six years. No two facets of the temple are the same: every convolution of every scroll is different. No two canopies in the whole building are alike, and every part exhibits a joyous exuberance of fancy . . .' Here too the guide looking at us, and not at the wall, keeps saying, 'That's Krishna dancing on the hood of the giant serpent Kalinga . . . See closely, you'll notice the Beauty being teased by the monkey, while she is dressing . . . Here is a man wearing a great coat with buttons. . . See the coiffure of this woman, does it not remind you of our modern fashions, which were really known 800 years ago? Do you observe this handmaid holding a mirror but looking away from her mistress—just to indicate the philosophy that one should not be vain . . .', and so forth. Rather a commonplace lesson he draws from all this work of art; but the guide is also, it seems to me, a part and parcel of life here, like the trees and hillocks and stones, with deep roots, irrespective of what he says, and I enjoy his voluble show.

SRAVANABELAGOLA

Sravanabelagola (57 km from Hassan) is the spiritual home of the Jain sect. Here Bhadrabahu, one of the immediate successors of Mahavira's personal disciples, died in a cave on Chandrabetta. With him came Chandragupta Maurya, who had renounced his throne and became a hermit. These events are assigned to the third century BC.

On Indrabetta, 1000 meters above sea level, was erected the statue of Gomateswara in 183 AD. 'The statues of this Jain Saint (Gomateswara),' says Fergusson, 'are among the most remarkable works of art in the south of India. One is astonished at the amount of labour such a work must have entailed, and puzzled to know whether it was a part of the hill or had been moved to the spot where it now stands. The former is the more probable theory. The hill is one mass of granite about 400 feet in height and probably had a mass or two standing on its summit—either a part of the subjacent mass or lying on it. This the Jains undertook to fashion into a statue 58 feet in height, and have achieved it with marvellous success. Nothing grander or more imposing exists anywhere out of Egypt and even there, no known statue surpasses it in height.'

CHIKMAGALUR

Fifty-five kilometers from Hassan is our next halt in the Emerald Circuit. Chikmagalur nestles in a valley south of Baba Buden Range, and looking about one sees the mountain ranges stretching away in serried ranks. An attractive hill town with its bright buildings, vast open spaces, its tree-covered slopes and parks, the centre for many coffee estates hinterland. The first generation of coffee plants of India was cultivated in this area. A Muslim saint, Baba Buden after whom the range of mountains is named, arrived from Arabia and settled in this mountainous country bringing with him a handful of coffee seeds; he planted them for his own use around his tabernacle, and this was the beginning of coffee cultivation in India, and one has to salute the memory of this saint for the lasting gift he brought us. The cave containing his tomb is at a deviation on the ghat road to Kemmangundi, sacred both to Muslims and Hindus, and known as Dattatreya Peeta. It is believed that Dattatreya disappeared into this cave and will reappear when Vishnu incarnates next as *Kalki* avatar to redeem the world.

Kemmangundi (64 km from Chikmagalur) is reached through a winding ghat section after a four-hour drive from Chikmagalur, the road passing through coffee estates, over the edge of deep valleys, and at the base of towering precipices. Kemmangundi captures a traveller's heart at first sight, with its neat red road, hedged by luscious plants and ferns, foot tracks mysteriously cutting through them leading to grassy uplands, valleys, and forests. Here live officials and workers connected with the Mysore Iron and Steel Works (now called Visvesvaraya Iron & Steel Works), and officials of the Forest and Horticulture Department who tend the gardens and are in charge of the guest houses. The main activity here is the mining of iron ore by blasting the red mountain sides and loading them in trolleys which roll down on cables to Bhadravathi Iron Works, seventy-two kilometers below.

A co-operative store, a couple of shops, a dispensary and a row of workmen's quarters, beyond a sloping down, are the ingredients of this little mountain habitation (rather than name it 'town'). People who live here seem to be happy in this isolation, which is now and then enlivened with the presence of weekend revellers who arrive in bus-loads from the coffee estates and the industrial establishments in Shimoga and Bhadravathi, and who sometimes make the local citizens nervous as they knock on doors and carry on their revelry uninhibited. An old resident confessed rather ruefully, 'It is frightening sometimes as they come in great numbers and we have no police protection, unless we call them from Chikmagalur. It must be especially discouraging for those who come for a quiet holiday at the guest house, Dattatri Bhavan, which used to be the residence of the Maharaja of Mysore in old days.' According to this person, film-shooting companies are coming in greater numbers and cause much distraction to the local population. 'They also take up all the available space at the guest house, and normal tourists who may want a quiet holiday are likely to be turned away.'

The great event in their day is the arrival of a bus from Chikmagalur at noon going to Tarikere, which is the nearest town for shopping or to enjoy a movie at a couple of theatres there. Their attuned ears catch the arrival of a bus a mile away: the passengers waiting at the bus stand, with godly patience, stir themselves, happy to escape the isolation for a few hours, and return by the same bus in the evening.

Our guest house is a new one built on the topmost hill, a spacious, well-furnished building. We are in a room, one side walled with sheet glass, through which a full moon can be seen almost as if within touching distance, shining on a rock face looming up in the shadows. At dawn one observes that the looming shape is a reddish mountain wall. As the sun rises the fleecy, white mist, filling the valley to the brim, at first looking like ocean waves stilled in calm air, melts gradually revealing glimpses of fields far below in the valley as through a rent in the veil; gardens and undulating fields are revealed inch by inch as the mist melts; and one notices the presence of a family far off, husband and wife, and their child in a red sweater, perched on a promontory jutting out; the lady in her purple sari, looks like a flower bed herself at this distance; the child seems to be in ecstasy as he waves to a red bus, toy-size, crawling down the winding road far below. Little farm-steads dotting the fields in the valley, moss-covered rocks and tree tops, shimmer and glisten in the sun.

SRINGERI

Twelve centuries ago Sankaracharya was born at Kaladi (in Cochin) of parents who had been childless, but praying night and day for an issue. In answer to their prayer Shiva appeared in the guise of an old man, in a dream, and asked, 'Do you want numerous children who live to be a hundred but are dullards and evil-doers or only one who is exceptionally gifted, but will live with you only for a short time?' They chose the latter. And Sankaracharya was born, with only sixteen years as his allotted span of life. In his fifth year he underwent spiritual and other disciplines; in his eighth year he mastered the Vedas, Shastras and Puranas. And in his tenth year he renounced all worldly interests and became a *Sanyasi*. The rest of his life is the record of a World Teacher. Through his writings, debates, and talks, he propagated his *Advaita* philosophy—a doctrine which says that all that exists is a particle of a Universal Soul and merges in the end in that Soul. 'His was the task of ending the nightmare of separateness', says one of his commentators.

After travelling extensively from Kashmir to Cape Comorin, he arrived in Sringeri, which had already been sanctified by the presence of sages like Vasishta, Viswamitra, Vibhandaka, Kasyapa and others, who had had their ashrams in its forests, and spent their days in meditation in this tranquil setting of wooded mountains, watered by River Tunga, which is considered holier than any other river in the world.

Sankara was carrying with him the golden image of Sharada or Saraswathi, the Goddess of Knowledge and had been in search of the right place for installing the image. He stood on the right bank of the river absorbing the scene before him. At his feet Tunga was flowing, its water radiant in the midday sun. He beheld now a spectacle on the opposite bank which was significant; he felt convinced that he was at the end of his quest. A cobra had spread its hood and held it like an umbrella over a spawning frog, to protect it from the sun. 'This is the place!' Sankara said. 'Here is harmony, an absence of hatred even among creatures which are natural enemies."*

Sankara crossed the river, deciding to establish his mission at this little village. First he proceeded to build four guardian temples on the surrounding hillocks, which were to protect the village from dangers, diseases, and the forces of evil. On the eastern hillock he built a temple for Kalabhairava, on the west for Anjaneya, on the south for Durga, and on the northern for Kali. Poojas are still being continued at these temples.

There is a repose and tranquillity in the air. The river flows softly. Strolling along its edge I notice a group of young men with an elderly companion in their midst. They are bathing in the river, washing their clothes, and at the same time listening to the lecture their elderly companion is giving them and answering questions put to them. When they get up to go, muttering their lessons, I follow them through the narrow passage behind the consecrated tombs of ancient saints.

I follow them into a large hall where groups of students are squatting in shady corners, quietly chanting their lessons and memorizing. A few scholars, wrapped in shawls, move about softly, absorbed in their own discussion.

---

* This sounds more a symbolic statement than a fact. I have heard similar reports at other temples in the course of my travel, with occasional variations. If it was not a cobra and frog, it would be a tiger protecting a lonely calf. Even at Sringeri, when I visited it some years ago, the spot on the river was marked by a niche made of a couple of rough stones; this niche was covered with mud and sand but a slight excavation with one's finger revealed a stone surface on which a cobra and frog were faintly etched. Now the spot is marked by a properly built mini-shrine with a realistic statue of cobra with its hood raised.

In the upper storey there is a library containing over four thousand manuscripts and books, neatly classified, labelled and arranged in glass shelves. In an adjoining room pundits are seated before heaps of manuscripts and books, examining a vast store of literary material that has accumulated in the *math* from time immemorial.

In the central courtyard there is a shrine, fittingly enough, of Sankaracharya. This is a college run by the *math*, providing a course of studies that extends over ten years; and here young men are being trained for a religious and priestly life. Once a year the pupils are examined and the successful candidates are led by their masters across the river to the presence of the chief guru, the apostolic head who lives on the other side of the river. He is a man of deep learning and austerity, whose hours are occupied in meditation, prayer, worship and studies. He tests the candidates himself, and distributes to them clothes and money.

There is a *Sanyasi* sweeping the temple of Anjaneya and decorating the image with flowers, completely absorbed in his work, and indifferent to those passing by him. To my inquiry my guide answers: 'He is one of the four of five *Sanyasis* here. He speaks to no one. He came here some years ago. We don't know where he has come from. He spends most of his time in yoga; occasionally when he is free, he sweeps the temples. Since he is here he is our guest.' I observe two *Sanyasis*, sitting on the river-steps, in the shadow of a banyan tree, with their eyes closed. They look disembodied souls in the pink glare of the setting sun. Their purpose is also unknown. One of them, it was vaguely understood, came all the way from the Himalayas in order to discuss certain metaphysical questions with the chief guru. But he never met the guru, but just stayed on, dividing his time between meditation and service. He voluntarily teaches certain subjects in the college, where another *Sanyasi* is a pupil. No one questions who they are or why they are here, but treats them as honoured guests. Sringeri acts as host to whoever visits it. The moment you arrive, you are freed from all concerns of food and shelter. You are shown a room in the Guest House, and then your hot water is ready for your bath, and as soon as you have bathed, your food is brought to you. There is an old cook, bent with age, who gets up every morning at four o'clock, and goes to bed at eleven in the night, spending his waking hours in serving guests. Every day hundred of visitors are being fed by the *math*, not counting the pupils in the university, the *Sanyasis*, and others. This hospitality is not confined to human beings. In the niches of the temple towers live thousands of pigeons. From the stores of the *math*, large quantities of corn are scattered in the courtyard; it is fascinating to watch the birds sweep down to feed at their hour. Rice is cooked and dumped in the river for the fish also. Numerous fish of all sizes, mostly dark blue in colour, sporting and splashing about, come to the surface expectantly whenever a human being approaches the river-step.

There are numerous temples in Sringeri besides the chief one of Sharada. The temple of Vibhandaka in Sringeri itself and of his son Rishvasringa, which is at Kigga, six miles from Sringeri, built on a high hill, are two of the oldest temples here. Both are of the same type with an inner shrine in the middle, an open corridor around, and a roofed platform on the edge of the corridor. The platform can accommodate thousands of persons at a time. It is believed that by praying at these temples rain can be called or stopped. Vibhandaka and his son are famous sages mentioned in the early portions of the Ramayana. Rishvasringa, like his father, was a man of great attainment, but he had grown up without ever having seen a woman. At that time there was a severe drought in Anga; the king was told that the drought would cease if Rishyasringa could be brought to his country and married to the princess. A bevy of young women disguised as hermits were sent in order to entice this sage. They arrived, stopped at Narve, a village near Sringeri, waited for an opportunity and came before the young man when his father was away. He felt such a deep interest in these strange hermits that it was not very difficult for them to decoy him. His approach to Anga brought rain. He married the princess and became the priest of King Dasaratha of Ayodhya, and officiated at the great sacrifice which resulted in the birth of Rama, the hero of Ramayana. There is a carving on a pillar in the Rishyasringa temple at Kigga in which the young sage is shown as he is being carried off happily on a palanquin made of the intertwined arms of fair women.

Another important temple is Vidyasankara's built in about 1357 AD. It is on the left bank of Tunga, of Chalukyan style, and built on a raised terrace. The unique feature of the temple is its pillared hall. The pillars are so placed that the first ray of the sun comes through the small eastern doorway, and unfailingly falls only on a particular pillar to indicate the zodiacal sign of the day, each of the twelve pillars representing one particular zodiacal position. The architect and the astronomer have combined to produce a masterpiece of precision, valid for ever. Round the outer walls are intricate carvings depicting scenes from the epics and puranas. One of the most interesting groups of figures is that of Vyasa and Sankara. This perhaps illustrates the episode in Sankara's life when sage Vyasa came to him in the guise of an old man when Sankara was teaching a group of disciples on the banks of Ganga. Sankara was teaching them Brahma Sutra of which Vyasa himself was the author. Vyasa objected to Sankara's interpretation of his work, but Sankara would not accept his view. A great debate ensued which went on for seventeen days, neither side giving in. At this the others grew alarmed. Sankara's chief disciple appealed to them to cease. And the debate was stopped. Vyasa blessed Sankara for his grasp of the subject and his interpretation. And as Sankara was about to complete his sixteenth year in a couple of hours, Vyasa blessed him with a further span of sixteen years of life.

*

The temple of Sharada is the holiest sanctuary one could be privileged to enter, the centre round which the life of Sringeri revolves. At the evening hour of worship the temple is transformed with lights, music, incense, and flowers. At this moment the golden image of Sharada in the innermost shrine, shining in the lamp-light and the swaying flames of camphor, appears as a living presence, and one feels one could go on standing here for ever looking at its tranquil and distinguished face.

Across the river, on the opposite bank, a five-minute ferrying in a long canoe-like craft, takes us to Narasimha Vana where resides the apostolic head of the *math*. The river flows on with a soft swish in the dark night; people are waiting on the banks to be taken across; some of the experienced crossers of the river utter a shrill cry which summons the ferry-man to come up from the other side. No seats are provided in the boat; one has either to stand and balance on one's feet, or squat on one's heel clutching the sides of the boat. I find both a difficult trial since my knee-joints have lost their flexibility owing to habits of occupying raised furniture. But this problem does not bother others who crouch in the canoe without discomfort, since they are used to sitting, with ease, for hours on the floor in the presence of the guru. Leaving the boat, the central building is to be reached through a garden of flowers and wooded area and reputed to be snake-infested; God knows what might be lurking under those dry leaves covering the path to the building. I feel a little nervous at the thought, but no one else is afraid since there has been no mishap at any time.

In the prayer hall are men and women, sitting on the floor to watch the pooja performed by the swamiji himself at night; he is the thirty-fifth guru coming in a single unbroken line from Sankara himself since the twelfth century. He is the custodian of the images of Ganesha and Shiva which were worshipped by Sankara himself, and he continues the pooja with offerings and rites as it was performed nearly one thousand years ago, while a group of men are chanting the *Rudra* mantras.

AGUMBE

This hill town, about 32 km from Sringeri, bordering South Kanara, is one of the highest points in Western

Ghats. The road leading to it is overhung with immense trees and passes through one of the densest forest regions in Karnataka. From a platform on a ledge, one could enjoy a bird's-eye view of the plains of South Kanara stretching away 2000 feet below, and ending in a hazy horizon—where the Arabian sea line, hardly a couple of inches in width, shimmers and trembles like some live object, under a bright sun. At sunset, the changing colours and forms of the sun, sky, and the sea, in combination, provide a gorgeous spectacle.

It was here that Parasurama, the son of Jamadagni lived. Jamadagni possessed a cow, given to him by Indra, the Cow of Plenty, called Surabhi, which could yield anything its owner desired. Kartavirya, who has a thousand arms and superhuman powers and oppressed both men and gods, tried to seize the cow. On hearing of his attempt, Parasurama chopped off his thousand arms and head with his famous axe. At this the sons of Kartavirya killed Jamadagni, whereupon his wife Renuka ascended the funeral pyre and immolated herself. With her dying breath she cursed her husband's murderers. Parasurama vowing to fulfil her curse, completely wiped out the warrior race, Kshatriyas, from the earth with his axe which had been given him by Shiva himself.

He cleared the earth of Kshatriyas twenty-one times and then performed a 'Horse Sacrifice' to commemorate his victory. Sage Kasyapa officiated as his priest at the sacrifice and was offered the earth itself as his fee. The sage accepted the fee and ordered Parasurama off his 'territory', which was the whole .earth. This was a ruse to get rid of Parasurama and save the remaining few Kshatriyas, without whom there would be no one to protect and rule the earth. Parasurama stood before the ocean and appealed to the God of Ocean to grant him a little space; in response to his appeal, the ocean rolled back, and thus were created South Kanara and the coastal districts along the Arabian Sea. Though the exact place of Parasurama's actions is undefined and is consequently claimed along the whole coast, my guide at Agumbe was certain that it was here, in these magnificent forests that Parasurama had his *ashram* and that the sea was at one time laving the side of the mountain on which we were standing.

MANGALORE

A sea-level, undulating country, hilly prospects, and with the Arabian Sea bounding the western limits. From early times, Mangalore has had contacts with the outside world and consequently, it has maintained an atmosphere of cosmopolitanism. As early as 1342 Ibn Batuta stated that he had noticed the presence of merchants from Persia and Yemen in the area. In 1448 Abdur Razak, ambassador from Persia, landed at Mangalore on his way to Vijayanagar. In 1498 Vasco da Gama landed in an island off Udipi coast. The city abounds in temples, churches and mosques—a result of the variety of influences that have made Mangalore what it is today. Historically speaking every nation or ruler has attempted to hold his sway over Mangalore; the Bednur Nayaks possessed it at first, in 1526 the Portuguese took it over, and for some reason they destroyed the city twenty years later, rebuilt it and burnt it down again. In 1670 the Portuguese were permitted to build a factory in Mangalore. Twenty-five years later the Arabs set fire to the city resenting the Portuguese authority there. Early in the eighteenth century the Portuguese were evicted by the Nayaks of Bednur, but in 1714 they were allowed to build their factory again. Haidar Ali took Mangalore in 1763; captured by the English in 1768, Tippu Sultan seized it in 1794, and after the fall of Srirangapatna, Mangalore came back to the British.

Naturally, with such constant attack, collapse, revival and incursions, a place gets notched. There had been four fortresses of importance within the city limits of Mangalore, built or destroyed by the Nayaks, Tippu Sultan, the Portuguese and the British by turns. Of these the remains of only the fort built by Basavappa Nayak (1740-54), and St. Sebastian built by the Portuguese stand witness to their times. A section of the moat, which surrounded the Mangalore fort, is still visible, and the relic of Sebastian Fort is the site on which stands a tile factory. Sultan Battery (Tippu's) and the Light House hill are other landmarks of history. Of the temples, Mangaladevi temple is the most important one built in the tenth century (the city is said to be named after this Goddess). Besides the Mangaladevi's, there are over ten other temples in the city. Manjunatha resides at Kadri Hill. There are also churches, St. Joseph's Theological Seminary, the church of the Most Holy Rosary at Bolar—one of the oldest churches of South Kanara founded in 1526, the St. Aloysius College Church, 1885, designed in the style of the Orator of St. Philip Neri in Rome, which displays a remarkable series of paintings on the wall and ceiling representing biblical subjects, done by Br. Anthonion Moschemi who had come from Italy in the year 1889.

Among the mosques rank the Jumma Masjid in the Bunder, built several centuries ago by the Arabs; the Idgha Mosque at the Light House Hill said to have been constructed by Tippu Sultan at the end of the eighteenth century. The Shamir Mosque at Dongerekery is two centuries old enshrining the tomb of the Saint, Shah Amir.

The construction of Mangalore all-weather harbour is a major undertaking, and will, in course of time, revolutionize the Karnataka trade pattern. Nearby is the Mangalore Fertilizers and Chemicals, one of the most important enterprises in Kamataka.

DHARMASTHALA

From Mangalore at a distance of 67 kilometers, tucked away from the main road beyond groves of arecanut and coconut palms. Difficult to classify it as a town or a village, with its native population of about 6,000, and a floating one of several hundred pilgrims each day, consisting mainly of Jains and Hindus and sometimes Muslims too. Whoever seeks God's grace to overcome suffering of any kind, comes here to pray. This is one place free from the barriers of caste or creed. The handbook of this Kshetra advises every pilgrim, 'While remaining in this *Kshetra*, he should spend the time in meditation, repetition of God's names, Bhajans, reading of sacred books, and as far as possible luxuries, comforts, aimless talks, arguments and vain discussions, should be avoided.' This could be a general prescription for anyone, any time, and any place, but at Dharmasthala, it has the force of an injunction. Religious life and the pursuits therefore are a serious business here.

Dharmasthala is a meeting point of Jains, Hindus, and sometimes Christians and Muslims too, and among the Hindus no differences are felt among Vaishanavas, Saivaites and Madhvas. In the Shiva temple, the priests are Madhva Vaishanavites, and Heggade is the *dharmadhikari* of all temples, although a Jain.

About five centuries ago, one Beemana Pergade, a Jain chieftain of this district, and his wife were vouchsafed a vision, while they were praying at Chandranatha Basadhi. The guardian goddess of Dharma and her spouse commanded Pergade to leave the house in which they lived, called *Neeyada Bheedu*, for the gods to occupy, and build another one for his family. (One could still see the original house in which Pergade used to live, now a shrine visited exclusively by the Heggade family for worshipping their ancestors as well as the guardian gods of Dharma.) The divinities again appeared in their dreams and commanded them to build shrines for Manjunatheswara, and other gods: they also indicated that one Annapa would be their channel of communication. Annapa fetched the Manjunatha in the form of *Linga* from Kadri and installed it. In further visions the Pergades were directed to conduct regularly festivals and poojas at the shrines, and to treat whoever visited Dharmasthala as their guests. Since that day, Dharmasthala has developed, everything being organized to meet the needs of pilgrims who arrive in a steady stream each day. Anyone who sends a postcard mentioning the time and date of his arrival will be received and given a room at one of the guest houses which are well furnished and equipped, with double rooms for larger families. Any guest can stay for three days free of charge, and take his seat in a long hall to be served food at dinner time. The Commissariat at Dharmasthala reminds one of the descriptions one had read in the puranas of the arrangements made during Shiva's marriage to Parvathi (Meenakshi), where food and delicacies of every kind were conjured up in mountainous quantities to feed a million guests and gods. We were taken through the building where provisions were stored. A pile of pumpkins was rolling off the back of a truck, other trucks also bringing in vegetables and coconuts on a similar scale; rice-bags, pulses and corn were stacked up to the ceiling; rows and rows of women, sitting along a corridor, winnowing and sorting the foodgrains. Every item is stored in perfect order and is accounted for; in the kitchen gigantic cauldrons are set over ovens packed with forest wood, capable of cooking a quintal of rice at a time, along with other items on the same scale—such as vegetables and lentils and sauce, and stirred with huge ladles. Every day and all the year round this arrangement has to go on, and the organization for it works smoothly, without hesitation, or anxiety, or shortage of any kind. Their explanation as to why they are so successful is simple; they are only executing the commands of the Devas of Dharma, who have assured them of resources and wealth without limit. Dharma has a wide connotation, applicable to many other aspects beside charity. It also means truthful adherence to a code or discipline, and everyone here performs his duty without any compulsion other than the inner one, and things always go right. There has been no theft of any kind in Dharmasthala. One seems to shed one's irritations and angularities while crossing the river Netravathi, which runs a mile and a half east of Dharmasthala.

The Heggades of Dharmasthala (coming in the line of Beemana Pergade) have continued as the heads of all the institutions here, generation after generation. A Heggade is the sole authority of this entire institution and is responsible for the maintenance of Dharmasthala. In addition to tending pilgrims the Heggades have been responsible for the starting of educational institutions, a mobile hospital, and other measures of social welfare and improvement. Heggade is the final arbiter in all civil strifes too; he listens to disputants regularly at the temple, and his decision is final and binding as he is the spokesman of Dharma Devas. Another area of their public service lies in helping any poor person to perform the marriage of his daughter. On an application, the chief arranges, absolutely without any expense to the parties, and without the omission of any of the religious rites, the wedding ceremony. Four hundred mass marriages were performed on an auspicious day in April 1976. I have preserved the invitation card sent out on this occasion as a unique souvenir. Dharma is a concept of wide, versatile applicability in the service of mankind, without any limit, at this abode of the gods of Dharma. The present head of Dharmasthala is Veerendra Heggade, who is young and was studying for his BA degree at Bangalore when he was suddenly called to take up the administration of Dharmasthala on the death of his father, Ratnavarma Heggade. A feat achieved in his time is the installation of Gomateswara Statue, at the highest point in Dharmasthala; the statue weighing ten tons, was transported 74 kms from Karkal (where the sculptor had worked on it for five years), hauled over hills and difficult terrain, by means of special trolleys and other mechanisms.

UDIPI

Seat of Madhvacharya (thirteenth century), one of the three great religious leaders of India, the others being Sankara and Ramanuja. He expounded the *Dwaita* philosophy as opposed to *Advaita* of Sankara. The *Dwaita* philosophy postulates a separate Individual Soul and a Supreme Being, as opposed to the position taken by Sankara that the Individual Soul and the Universal Soul are not different entities. Madhvacharya was born in 1238 at Pajakakshetra on the outskirts of Udipi (9 kms.) and lived to be seventy-nine. He was a profound thinker and scholar and has left about thirty-six works in Sanskrit expounding his philosophy, and also interpreting Upanishads, Vedanta Sutras, Bhagavad Gita, etc. His writing had a profound effect on his generation, and the succeeding ones. He asserted that the world was real and not an illusion (no *Maya*); he explained that there are five distinctions that are eternally present: between God and Man; between God and Matter; between Soul and Matter; between one Soul and another; between Matter and Matter; this was dualism complete leaving no scope for identity in any form. His emphasis was on the value of Bhakthi. He travelled widely propagating his philosophy and mission all over the country, and engaging himself indefatigably in debates with other scholars and philosophers and vanquishing many an opponent in such encounters. In addition to his spiritual and intellectual strength he was reputed to be endowed with super physical strength (being the son of Vayu, who was the progenitor of both Hanuman and Bhima, both of whom possessed immeasurable power), and humbled the pride of the sturdiest wrestlers of his time.

He also performed miracles—not to impress others but to bring relief and peace to anyone undergoing any kind of suffering. He established eight centres and appointed his disciples to be in charge of each. The Udipi Jain *math* is the central one with its temple of Krishna, which image Madhvacharya had discovered in a lump of yellow clay given by the captain of a ship, which was in distress off the coast of Udipi, but was saved by Madhva's miraculous powers. The impact of Madhva's philosophy brought forth a number of scholars and spiritual seers—Vadhiraja, Jayateertha, Vyasateertha, Raghavendrateertha, and Vijayadhwaja; and also a number of composers and minstrels, the most famous among whom were Purandara Dasa and Kanaka Dasa, of a class broadly called 'Haridasas'. Their compositions were in Kannada, an outpouring of their joy in the contemplation of God Krishna. The temple at Udipi attracts pilgrims from all over India. Krishna's image is beautiful, fully decked in gold and diamonds, to be viewed through perforations in the door of the sanctum, for which darshan, there is always a line of devotees, who peep in at the shrine for a few seconds and move on. Poojas are performed without any deviation as they were performed centuries ago, at the appointed hours from morning till late night with elaborate rituals. The several festivals celebrated all through the year bring in many visitors from the surrounding country. The most important of the festivals falls on the third week of January of even years when the Swami in charge of the administration hands it over to the next in rotation. The eight *maths* established have their headquarters at the temple precincts themselves, and the heads of these *maths* take charge of the administration by turns. One interesting legendary point here is the 'Kanaka

Dasa Kindi', a peep hole in the main door through which Kanaka Dasa, who could not enter the temple owing to his caste, is said to have had a darshan of Krishna, whose image in the sanctum turned from east to west in order to afford him a view.

The swamijis of the eight *maths* are enlightened men, deeply spiritual and learned, but they have not overlooked the temporal values needed for a society. Under their patronage many colleges and educational institutions have been established at Udipi.

PAJAKAKSHETRA

Birthplace of Madhvacharya. An image of Madhva was set up in a shrine at the spot of his birth more than five hundred years ago, and one can still visit various places in this charming village where the great master lived and played and even exhibited his extraordinary powers as a child. The house where the saint was born is beside two hillocks; on one hill is a temple of Chamundi, as Mahishasura Mardhini, whom Madhvacharya worshipped. A tranquil hamlet where the saint spent his childhood and formative years, dividing his time between inquiry, contemplation, writing, and clmbing the little hill to worship at the shrine every day. When the time came, he went out and discovered his Guru at Udipi and decided to become a *Sanyasi*. The other hill has many caves with ponds, enough retreats for one in whom sainthood was germinating.

SUBRAMANYA

To continue the Emerald Circuit, leaving Mangalore for Mercara a slight detour, and through the most imposing ghat roads and a descent at some point we reach Subramanya, at a distance of 104 km from Mangalore. It is between two peaks, Kumara Parvatha and Sesha Parvatha, in a basin, where a little river named Kumaradhara flows, on the banks of which there is the original shrine of Subramanya in the form of a mud ant-hill. God Subramanya is worshipped here in his serpent form. Prayers are directed to this God for protection from the poisonous effects of any reptile bite from all over the country. Everything about this place has a serpent background and association. On one's way from the temple to Kumaradhara there is a sacred spot named Biladwara in which hid Vasuki the king of serpents, fearing an attack from Garuda; it has many tunnels and passages, and some are impassable with jungle growth and teeming with unseen, unclassifiable creatures. A mountain peak looming on the east of the temple is said to be about nineteen kilometers away, rising to a height of 1230 meters without a road. Anyone who can face the hazards of mountain climbing may go up on this adventure and at the thirteenth kilometer he will see a *mantapa* with carved pillars. What sculptor could have come up here, one will wonder, but one is told of the relics of farms and homes—also to be seen—at least five hundred years old, giving one an inkling, but no more than an inkling, of an ancient township. Onward it is said to be steeper, a vertical wall of rock, impossible to climb. This forbidding elevation somehow also fascinates one, and one wishes one were younger to face the challenge of this mountain beyond dense forests. One faces three peaks, which, I am told by those who have ventured thus far, give an impression of a seven-hooded serpent. Every association here is serpentish. If one has the hardihood to proceed along, one could reach the proximity of Siddha Parvatha, declared totally inaccessible to human beings, but Vishnutirthacharya (brother of Madhva and head of Sode Mutt in his days), retreated there five hundred years ago and is believed to be there still in meditation. An air of whispered sanctity and mystery envelops one at every step. On another peak called Kumara Parvatha, at the end of a strenuous climb one will be rewarded with the spectacle of footprints carved on stone; the legendary account of it being that at this spot the coronation of God Kumara (or Subramanya) took place, and the holy water after the rituals, flowed in two different directions, named Ubhaya and Kumaradhara, separately as two rivers and merged beyond Subramanya. The ground is strewn with quartz crystals of different sizes, but of the same symmetry, occasionally in the form of *linga*, to be treasured by the finder as a divine souvenir. From this point one could have a panoramic view westward of South Kanara's fertile forests and fields, Coorg and its estates on southeast, and the plains of Mysore northeast. God Kumara ever loves to reside on inaccessible mountain tops all over South India and here he has chosen a terrain dearest to His heart. This little village named after the God, and its shrine with a few scattered habitations and shops around is unimpressive at first sight, but viewed against its background of legend and soaring mountains and forests, the place assumes enormous dimensions.

MERCARA

The ghat road to Mercara winds through forests and tree tops edging the road, with their trunks going endlessly down the valley; if you peep over the edge of the road, or take a step on the slope which gets lost in the thicket and foliage, you get a feeling that you may never be seen again. Rubber trees with plastic bags stuck on their sides, as well as Cocoa plantations are in evidence as you pass Sullia. While entering the borders of Coorg, one becomes aware of passing into an absolutely original and special kind of country. There are several historical, geographical and ethnic reasons for the difference one notices in Coorg. Life in Coorg is conditioned by a mountain climate and its terrain, and people's occupation, mainly outdoor, in plantations, fields, and forests. Coffee, spices such as pepper, cardamom, and cloves, orange and other citrus variety, and honey are the chief produce, and also timber from the forests. Men and women are hard-working and relax happily during a festival, such as Tula Sankramanam or during a wedding celebration; their marriage customs are unlike those in other parts of the country, and celebrated with dance, song and feasting. Coorgs are a martial race,* robust and hardy, enjoying physical activity, and every kind of outdoor life. The town square of Mercara is presided over by a statue of General Thimmaya.

---

* The Coorgs are an ancient North Indian or Indo-Scythian race, who came down South and settled in Coorg under circumstances which the historians are not able to unravel. They came as immigrants and absorbed the local language and culture to a certain extent, but without losing their original customs and ceremonies.

General Cariappa's home is pointed out to the visitor with pride. Apart from the generals, men from Coorg have served the country in many ways, and their extrovert and sportive nature are endearing qualities. A little reference to history will help us to understand how Coorg has been shaped. The earliest mention of Coorg is found in Tamil literature of the Sangam period. The Tamil poets while extolling the Pandyan rulers and the extent of their territory mention 'Kudakam' as the western boundary of their territory and the Bay of Bengal as the eastern. Coorg, up to the seventh century was not ruled by any single ruler but by a number of chieftains, each carving up and ruling a territory, deriving his authority from one or the other of some bigger outside power. Only inscriptions give us any information of Coorg up to the sixteenth century. The Ganga kings who ruled from Talkad from the third century, probably held Coorg also under their suzerainty. The southern half of Coorg must have been under them. From the tenth century, Changalvas, who were probably hill chieftains, ruled Southern and Central Coorg, and they were feudatories of the Gangas; the northern parts of Coorg were under the Kadambas for some time. With the overthrow of the Gangas by Cholas in the tenth century, the Cholas became dominant in Mysore and the northern parts of Coorg, for over a hundred years. The Cholas mention Kudu Malainad among their conquered territories, which means 'Coorg Hill Country'. With the rise of Hoysalas of Dwarasamudra the Chola suzerainty ended in the Kannada country. In the fourteenth century, when the Muslim powers from Delhi invaded the South, the Hoysalas along with other Hindu dynasties were overthrown. The Vijayanagar Empire extended upto

Coorg about this time. In the fourteenth, fifteenth and sixteenth centuries, Coorg was being ruled by petty chiefs called Nayakas who had each carved out their own spheres of authority and power, and were at constant war with each other, which facilitated the entry of a third power in the shape of a prince of Ikkeri family from Shimoga. In 1791 the British declared war on Tippu Sultan with the Coorg Rajas as their allies. Both Haidar Ali and then Tippu had constantly menaced the Coorg rulers and so when an opportunity arose, the Coorg rulers promptly acted for their own survival.

Virarajendra, who had been incarcerated with his entire family for six years in the Periapatna Fort and later escaped and organized his army to fight the garrisons established in different parts of Coorg by Tippu, negotiated with the British successfully for an alliance. General Abercromby who was the British Commander, first met Virarajendra, for talks at a place later immortalized by the Raja in his own name, as Virarajendrapet (or Virazpet), which today is next to Mercara in importance. Virarajendra continued to be friendly with the British residents and governors; but after his death, his successors became rather hostile and in 1832 the British deposed the Raja and annexed Coorg; on the 6th of April 1834 the British flag was hoisted on the fort at Mercara. Under the British rule, the economic and agricultural conditions improved; coffee cultivation was encouraged on a large scale. The Coorgs proved loyal to the British, and in appreciation of their loyalty and help in quelling sporadic local revolts and uprisings, Sir Mark Cubbon allowed the citizens of Coorg to own arms personally and individually while in all other parts of India, the Arms Act was strictly enforced, and no one could own any weapon without a licence. When India became independent, Coorg was classified as a 'Part C' State, but following the reorganization of states, on linguistic basis, Coorg became a district of Karnataka.

Mercara, the capital city of Coorg, has a population of 14,453 according to the census of 1961. Mercara today is a pleasant little town; wherever you turn you are enchanted by the picture of wooded slopes, homesteads in the little valleys, and the undulating landscape.

We are staying at Sudarsan Guest House, which was formerly the British Resident's mansion, with large halls and bedrooms, a spacious and graceful old building, verandas and windows opening on green terraces, flower beds, winding roads and trees. It is very interesting to walk along the bazaar street, with cars and buses passing (Coorg is connected only by buses with the outside world). The former palace of the Rajas was rebuilt by Lingaraja II in 1812-14, according to a metal plaque on the wall within the fort, which originally had been built by Tippu and named Jaffarabad, and seized by Virarajendra in 1790; at another end of the fort is Omkareshwara temple built by Lingarajendra in 1820. It is said that Lingaraja built it as atonement for his hasty act in ordering the execution of a pious brahmin. In front of the temple there is a sky-blue tank, calm and unruffled. Other spots to which one is guided are the Rajas' tombs, where lie Virarajendra and his successors and members of the royal family. A place called the Raja's Seat at the other end of the town is an elevated plateau with gardens and lawns and a mantap, where the Raja used to sit down to gaze on the endless vista of valleys, fields and slopes far off. A sinister reputation is also attached to this 'Seat'; enemies of the Raja were supposed to be hurled down the most precipitous part of this hill, while he watched, but this is unsubstantiated, and seems to be only a morbid speculation.

*

We drive fifty kilometers out of Mercara, through Bhagamandala, and reach Talakaveri on the slopes of Brahmagiri Hill, the birthplace of River Kaveri, which wells up as a modest spring within a little trough, flows down through Coorg and Mysore up to Sivasamudram, from where it precipitates itself into Tamil Nadu and joins the sea in Tanjore area, nourishing human life and plant life for hundreds of kilometers all along the way. We are at a height of 125 meters above sea level, and fortunate to be here on the eve of a very important day. Tomorrow at a precise moment, at 7.40 a.m., astrologically calculated and fixed, when the sun enters Libra, Kaveri will be born. At that exact moment in the little trough-like structure above a larger tank, the river's birth will take place in the form of a little bubble rising to the surface, and then a larger one, and gradually more and more until the water will rise in a spout a couple of feet high, the moment for which the public will be waiting. To be able to obtain a sprinkling of water at that moment on one's head confers benediction. From all over the country crowds have started pouring in, prepared to brave the night, so cold and windy at this height, to camp at night in order that they may not miss the auspicious moment in the morning; they arrive in buses, taxis, and on foot trudging up the six kilometers from Bhagamandala. In order to regulate the movement of traffic from Bhagamandala, the police are employing walkie-talkies.

Already crowds have thronged here and many preliminary rites are going on at the tank. Priests are lighting camphor at the little water-filled trough which is actually a shrine of Goddess Kaveri. Packets and packets of *kumkum* are handed to the priests by devotees, to be emptied into the trough with *mantras*; the trough has become completely red with all that quantity of *kumkum* dissolved in it. All kinds of activities are going on here almost twelve hours ahead of the Sankramanam. People are wading, dipping, and splashing about, ecstatically, in the tank below the spring. Several priests seated beside the shrine are performing their Sandhya prayers, oblivious of the pressing crowd around. Babies are held down and given a ducking, as they shiver in the cold; men with shaved heads swim along like fish under and above the water, and reach the trough where the priest in attendance pours red *kumkum* water over their heads out of a bowl—wave after wave of shaven heads are presented up for this favour from the priests and then climb the steps and dry themselves and wear their clothes, completely ignoring the teeth-chattering cold. Another group of shaven men is busy lighting little wicks in the hollow of coconuts and floating them off on water. A batch of girls stands on the steps and sings a chorus in praise of Kaveri. Bells are ringing continuously. All sorts of activities seem to go on simultaneously. Everyone is happy and expectant, totally unmindful of the cold air, exposure and the lack of accommodation. Policemen lean on the parapet and keep a watch, a good number of them are concentrated here, and many more along the way down to Bhagamandala and Mercara, since huge crowds are already swarming up, and tomorrow at least fifty thousand if not a hundred thousand pilgrims are expected to arrive in time to touch the sacred waters of Kaveri.

And then on our way back to Mysore, pausing for a few hours at Nagarahole Game Sanctuary. After lunching in a cottage set amidst teak plantations and in the shade of gigantic rose-wood trees, we set out in a car through the forest paths, obeying all the rules prescribed for watching wild life: to observe silence, not to gesticulate, and to remain, for ever, alert. Spotted deer in herds scamper, and bound away into thickets, two elephants at two different places stand aside like carved statues (similar to the sculptured life-size statues of two elephants one saw at the Mercara Fort), according to reports of other passengers in our car, although I was not smart enough to spot them out; bisons were seen crossing; we spent a long time hoisted on a platform which gave on a water-hole some four hundred meters away, where at dusk, the forest creatures are expected to gather. We stay on at the platform watching the edge of the pond, peering into the dusk, and whispering among ourselves, but nothing stirs, although if one is in luck one could see a tiger arrive for a drink of water; we are assured that there are sixteen tigers in this sanctuary, but one must have a special kind of luck in such matters; today we are not lucky, being a Sunday, there is too much of tourist traffic in jeeps and cars through the forest, and game unobtrusively retreat into inaccessible areas within these three hundred and odd kilometers of reserve.

On to Mysore through Hunsur; as we approach Mysore the sparkling lights outlining Chamundi Hill, ever a welcome sight, seem to beckon us on the completion of the Emerald Circuit.

Part Two

The Rockies

Gulbarga, Raichur, and Bidar came into Karnataka after the reorganization of states in 1956. Before that time they were in Nizam's territory. Before Nizam's, Gulbarga had been the Bahamani capital; earlier, it had been under the rule of Warangal Chiefs. For nearly 1500 years Gulbarga was prominent in the history and culture of the Deccan. Many of the ruling houses had their capital there. Rashtrakutas had their capital at Malkhed, 35 km from Gulbarga eastward. Kalyana, the capital of the later Chalukyas, formed part of Gulbarga district.

Gulbarga fort built by one Raja Gulchand at first and later developed by Alla-ud-din Bahamani, lies south of the town covering a vast ground. After a visit to the fort, the sort of conversation that takes place among the company:

'Which one was the second fort we saw this morning?

'There was no second fort, we saw only one . . .'

'No, after visiting Juma Musjid, did we not see a big fort with domes and terrace, where we went round and admired the lime concrete which had stood for so many years?'

'Yes, yes, I remember now. I am also beginning to wonder what it was, big gates, huge doors and gateways with three donkeys blocking the entrance, and a wide moat covered with water hyacinth with some persons fishing in those dark waters . . .'

Actually this discussion refers only to one fort, though creating an illusion of several. The fact is we have had a surfeit of fortresses ever since we left Hyderabad by road twenty-four hours ago, and they have telescoped in retrospect.

Yesterday we passed through Bidar, which became the capital of Bahamani kingdom after Gulbarga. One could well understand the rationale for this change. Bidar landscape is most attractive with its elevation (about 900 meters). Green fields, uplands, downs, and hill-ranges on the sky-line. From the eminence of our guest house we watch traffic in a valley, with bullock carts and villagers passing along of Lilliputian dimensions. A fort, mainly of red stone, dominates the landscape, commanding a view miles around. From its watch-towers one could spot out an enemy-column's approach even when it is far away. The side walls of the fortress are steep enough to discourage any attempt by the enemy to scale them. The town seems to have developed within the ramparts of the fort, with its streets, modern shops, and homes and business houses. Portions of the palace are still intact, with their high domes and lattice windows, partly accommodating government offices, and among them a 'Land-Records' office, with bundles stacked up to the ceiling, contains, as the officer explained, records which could be traced up to seventy-five years, which sounds rather tame against this great complex of fortresses and buildings and palaces standing for centuries. The most impressive spot here is the Madrassa, one of the earliest universities to teach Islamic religion and culture, with accommodation for over three hundred scholars and students, with its spacious quadrangle and dormitories and rooms on three floors, narrow stairways, started by Mohamed Gawan—a remarkable man who having run away from his home in Persia, ultimately found his way to this part of the world.

*

At Gulbarga the fort covers several hectares, wherein is situated the Jami Mosque, with 38,000 square feet of built-up space, in the style of the mosque at Cordova in Spain. Its entire roof is made up of a number of cup-shaped domes, supported on arched columns. The arches are so designed and placed that the speaker's dais is unobstructed from any part of the hall; this perhaps is responsible for the perfect acoustics of the hall; a low-voiced utterance from the speaker's platform can be heard clearly and naturally throughout the hall; not the whispering gallery type, but ordinary, normal conveyance of sound. When one stands here, one sighs for this lost art; we have now concert halls, built at a heavy cost, which are full of echoes and need special arrangements for muffling, and then loud-speakers in order to enable sound to reach all portions of the hall. I could not help thinking how successfully a music concert could be held in this hall without amplifiers, which has been the dream of the more sensitive among our artistes today. Also our builders should study in what manner, builders of those days could make lime mortar so smooth and lasting. It seems to me that at some point we have got disconnected from our traditions and techniques of building, and have become enslaved to the habit of using cement and steel for every purpose.

At the eastern part of the city, the tomb of Kwaja Bande Nawaz, an impressive mausoleum set in a courtyard which is cool and shady, with a pond under the branches of a spreading tree, where many worshippers and pilgrims are resting. Kwaja Bande Nawaz was born in Delhi in 721 Hijri, completed his education at the age of fifteen, became a disciple of Hazrath Khaja Pir Naseerudin Mahmood Chirag of Delhi and devoted all his time to philosophical studies and enquiry. After his master's death in 757 Hijri, Hazrath Kwaja Bande Nawaz, taking his place, continued his religious and spiritual work. When Delhi was threatened with Timur's invasion, he left Delhi and came to Gulbarga in the year 803 Hijri, at the invitation of the Bahamani ruler. Hazrath Kwaja Bande Nawaz remained in Gulbarga for twenty-two years and passed away in the year 825 Hijri. He had immense popularity, and influence on his admirers, irrespective of caste or community. He had profound scholarship, and equal felicity in Arabic, Persian and Urdu. The authorship of over a hundred books is attributed to him. He preached unity and universal brotherhood, and his devotion to the services of his fellowmen gave him a huge following in his days, and continues even now, after 568 years. The saint is at rest under a brocade-covering. With incense and flowers the visitors pay their respects to his memory. The great peace of death is felt in the air as also the immortality of the spirit at the same time. Brocades in green, the ancient lace drapes on the walls, and the fading paintings have a serene beauty. A library of ten thousand volumes in Arabic, Persian, and Urdu is preserved in a building within the high walls of the mosque. The annual *urs* attracts thousands of visitors; the Nizams in ancient days always camped here for the *urs*, staying at Ivan Shahi Palace (now a guest house where we were accommodated), and it is said that the Nizam's special train would be brought right up to the veranda outside his bedroom. Ivan Shahi Palace is set in a woodland of trees and flower gardens. The Divisional Commissioner's office is accommodated in a part of this building. Mahboob Garden maintained by the municipality is a public park, Nehru Ganj is the principal commercial centre. The shopping area is bright and lively.

Close to the Gulbarga Tank is built the shrine of Sharana Basaveswara. He was an eminent philosopher and teacher. Though the special occasion is the Jatra in Chitra Bahula, when a lakh of visitors congregate, even normally the temple is crowded with devotees, arriving from far and near. In Sharana Basaveswara's name colleges of arts and science, commerce and law have been established. Further educational facilities are provided, in Gulbarga, through well-equipped engineering and medical colleges.

*

We leave by road to reach Bellary the same evening. The sun beats down relentlessly like an arc-welding flame; the earth seems to be flat up to the horizon, the road stretches ahead with the dead-straightness of an arrow, flanked by acres of black cotton soil. We suddenly pass beside piled up, grim-looking bare rocks with obscure fortifications on their crest. At this hour the earth looks uninhabited. Hours pass before we come upon a village woman crossing a field with a child in arm. Large cattle-herd block our passage frequently, our driver desperately attempting to cut his way through, by sounding the horn and racing the engine. Again arrow-straight road ahead, black soil, and grim rocks flanking the road. The monotony of the spectacle lulls my senses, and I fall into a doze. Wake up to read the highway sign, 'Shahpur ends and Shorapur begins'; notice a stream flowing under a culvert, partly sand-covered, with village children standing waist-deep in a puddle. Also notice a motor cycle abandoned on the roadside. A man in a blue bush-coat standing at a road-corner waves us to a stop. He has been informed of our arrival and leads us, through a passage between boulders, to a bungalow on a hill-top. He is a 'Junior Engineer' in charge of 'minor irrigation', and the motor cycle we noticed on the way is his, suddenly broken down, and he manages somehow to get back to this branch road and wait for us. He is in charge of the guest house, which is a very attractive building overlooking the town, where Meadows Taylor lived a hundred years ago. As students we were familiar with his name, his 'Tara' and 'Confessions of a Thug' were our non-detailed study, and excellent reading in spite of their being text-books. Long forgotten, but delighted to be reminded of him in this remote town, and to be sipping coffee and resting in the building he had constructed. As a young man, he ran away from Liverpool and found his way to India, took on a small job in Bombay, and with one thing and another involved himself in the politics and wars taking place in this part of the country. Bedar Nayaks, whose capital was Shorapur, had held out against Aurangazeb at first, and then resisted the British rule in 1857. After their defeat, Shorapur State was administered by the British Commissioner from Hyderabad, and Meadows Taylor functioned as his agent at first, and later when it was made over to the Nizam of Hyderabad, Taylor became his representative. The only token of Taylor remaining in this house is the 'T' at various angles on the door and window frames, but his favourite chair, and his portrait in Rajasthani style, smoking hookah, were seen by us earlier at the museum in Gulbarga; his books are also kept there. This bit of literary associations at this remote place seems incredible. What an extraordinary link between Liverpool and Shorapur!

Shorapur town is eight square kilometers in area, situated on an elevated tableland with hills around. River Krishna flows eleven kilometers away, westward. Gopalaswamy Temple stands out prominently. Going through the town, I find that its most important landmark is the palace of the old Nayak Chieftains; a portion of the palace accommodates the local college. The Nayak's family continue, the sitting member of the Karnataka Legislature resides in a part of the palace and is a direct descendant of the dynasty that ruled here a couple of centuries ago. I always speculate how people spend their time in a pretty little place like this. The Junior Engineer explains that he loves this town, having lived here for three years; his professional duties keep him fully engaged. His family consists of his wife and three children, two of them of school-going age. While he is talking, I notice a row of children perched on the compound wall of a building holding on to themselves their aluminium school-boxes and water-bottles (school children lend a touch of universality, wherever they may be). The Junior Engineer explains that after his day's outing on inspection of the minor tanks, he is content to spend his time with the family at home. When he wants entertainment he takes his family to one or the other of the two cinema theatres in the town, or to the Gopalaswamy Temple, where the celebration of *Gokulashtami* festival is a seasonal event of much local interest. The sight of a black-coated lawyer standing at the bus stand hints at the possibility of courts and litigation and complicated activities in the background. The town has its quota of lawyers, doctors, and officials, and they have an evening club, but our Junior Engineer is quite content to spend the available hours with his family. I speculate on the possibility of this town and the Junior Engineer affording a theme for a short novel, of a world that looks minor but expands in retrospect as history, and in prospect as a centre of various modern developments; but at the moment, remaining a circumscribed community, with the peasant-class in the surrounding villages, living in a world of their own. In a geographically limited space, life is capable of acquiring great intensity.

We stop at Lingsugur for lunch. A village with only apparently a Block Development Office and a travellers' bungalow. One is surprised how a lunch could be produced here. But nowadays no place is too small to provide a furnished, comfortable rest house and food, since ministers and district officials are constantly on the move, attending to rural problems in the interior parts of the country.

On to Bellary, far far away, as it seems. Once again dead-level flat ground, black soil, and straight road to the horizon. We presently find our road flanked by rock formations of the weirdest type, gigantic pebbles strewn and kicked about by giants, and piled up precariously one on another with an occasional mysterious fort-wall on top. The stones have an abnormal look about them, gigantic pellets, with an unearthly dark sheen on their surface, scattered all over the fields; they fascinate—one cannot take one's eye off. We speculate on their legendary possibilities. Is this where Bhimasena had his lunch intended for *Bakasura*, and are these the pebbles he flung at the dogs approaching him for a morsel? Or were they left over after

Rama had reclaimed the ocean for crossing on to Lanka? Or could these be unknown Ahalyas cursed to be in this state for a moral lapse and awaiting redemption?

When we cross the Tunga Bridge the outlook changes. Green fields and fertile land, and cool air. The Tungabhadra project is transforming the land. We stop by at Sindhanoor, which is a new township, active and prosperous and with its shops and institutions and schools; it is unbelievable that no longer ago than ten years it was an arid, deserted village.

As we near Bellary, I have some regret that I could not detour to Malkhed, 38 km from Gulbarga, once a historic capital, flourishing under the Rashtrakutas in 757-953 AD. No vestige of the old glory is left today, I am told, still I love to sigh over ruins and monuments. Another point of interest at Malkhed is the Samadhi of Tikkacharya, an eminent Madhva saint, Jayateertha, who wrote commentaries (or Tikka) on Madhva's works. We were familiar with the name of Tikkacharya in our school days when we used to get an unexpected, unexplained, holiday for Tikkacharya *Punyadina*: and only after these many years, one understands whom we used to honour with a public holiday.

Reaching Bellary after nearly ten hours in the car was quite a welcome end of the journey. Once again sheltered in one of Nizam's palaces, now a guest house, a mansion with fifteen feet high arched doorways, very comfortably equipped, Bellary itself seems to me a forbidding town; its rocks with fortresses looming over the town, and a strange thorny shrub growing everywhere, unshapely and frightening, said to have been imported by some minister in the old days, from Australia to arrest soil erosion, but now flourishing as a pest, stretching out and ready to claw at you if you are not watchful at the roadside or a field.

A tour around the town and in spite of all its forbidding aspects, it is a well-developed town, a district which has been constantly changing hands. Bellary district, after the fall of Vijayanagar, was occupied by the Palaygars. In 1677 Shivaji wrested away the possessions of Bijapur rulers and visited Bellary district. In 1687 Aurangzeb acquired Bellary following his conquest of Bijapur and Golconda. In 1761 Haidar Ali moved through the Bellary region, and again seven years later to help the Nayak against the Subehdar of Deccan, and then later turned on the Nayak and demanded the surrender of his fort. And so on and on, with one power or another besieging until overpowered by another power, call them Mugals, Deccan Chiefs, Nayaks, Nawabs, Peshwas, or Palaygars, they were all at it at one stage or another, and after the fall of Tippu, Bellary finally passed into the hands of the British, being one of the Ceded Districts. In 1953 when the Andhra State came into being, Bellary with seven taluks was transferred to the old Mysore State.

Bellary today is a town of many educational institutions, medical, scientific, commercial and technical, and high schools. A steel plant of great dimensions is planned at Tornagal (28 km from Bellary), the Fifth Steel Plant, on an area of 4050 hectares, with the adjunct of a township to accommodate a population of five lakhs, and to produce, initially, two million tons of steel; the foundation for this project was laid in 1972. The economic and social life of Bellary is expected to change dramatically when this project is fulfilled. At the end of a long journey, to reach the Tungabhadra Dam and the Vaikunt Rest

House is an unbelievably luxurious experience. The Vaikunt is on a hillock (51 meters above sea level) and grants a view of the entire dam and the water-spread stretching over 376 square kilometers. My room has a large sheet glass giving on the dam side, and it is a rich moment when you watch the red sun tinting the water surface, poised like a red-hot disc over the horizon. Luckily for me this is the bright half of the month, and presently the opulence of moonlight is also over the water.

Tungabhadra is originally the Pampa River of the Ramayana. Tunga and Bhadra are two rivers which have their origin in the Western Ghats at a spot called Varaha Parvatha. Its legendary origin is that Vishnu assumed in one *avatar*, the form of a boar (varaha) and rescued the earth from a demon, and rested after his exertions on the mountain; when perspiration from the tusks dripped down, the right tusk was known as Bhadra and the left as Tunga, and the two streams flowing down the mountain merged at Kudali, eight miles from Shimoga, and came to be known as Tungabhadra.

VIJAYANAGAR

The Vijayanagar Empire was founded by Harihara and Bukka in 1336 and was established firmly by 1346. The Vijayanagar rulers established a firm administration and paid a great deal of attention to the welfare of their subjects, among other measures, by planning canal irrigation, which were so perfectly executed that those canals are still in use as a part of Tungabhadra Project network. Vijayanagar had a succession of good kings among whom Devaraya II and

Krishnadevaraya are famous. Devaraya was victorious in his encounters with the Andhra and the Bahamani kingdoms, and his influence had reached up to Ceylon. Krishnadevaraya had many brilliant military achievements to his credit, and his diplomatic relations with other rulers were also perfectly balanced. After his death, his successors proved weak and irresolute, and a new dynasty called Aravidu, founded by Krishnadevaraya's nephew and son-in-law, ruled for 100 years; in 1563 the Vijayanagar king, Ramaraca, proved a formidable opponent to the Bahamani Sultans; at some point the five sultans decided to combine their forces in order to check Ramaraca's progress. In 1565 the Battle of Talikotta was fought and brought to an end the Vijayanagar rule. Ramaraya was betrayed by two Muslim commanders who were in his service, and in the ensuing confusion, worsened by an elephant suddenly gone wild, Ramaraya's palanquin bearers deserted him and ran away. Ramaraya was captured by the enemy who cut off his head, and displayed it prominently on the battlefield: Ramaraya's followers were demoralized at this spectacle, were routed, and the capital was ravaged and destroyed.

HAMPI

Fourteen kilometers away from Tungabhadra Dam, is the site of the old Vijayanagar Empire at Hampi. One is subject to a feeling of both thrill and desolation when one visits this village. All the relics and monuments standing witness to an era of glory from the time of Harihara and Bukka, the founders of the dynasty, to the last King Ramaraya who lost his life and empire on the fields of Talikotta, are scattered over an area of 26 square kilometers. Theirs was an unparalleled achievement, in art, architecture, social organization, and military strength. One is thrilled at the memory of this phase of Vijayanagar history and desolate on reading the accounts of its downfall. One feels moved to great admiration at the sight of, for instance, the image of Ganesha standing twelve feet high, and shock at the sight of the damage inflicted on it. Ugra Narasimha, yet another instance of a large-hearted conception and execution. Twenty-two feet high, crowned with a seven-headed cobra, with Lakshmi on his lap, but alas, this is where one feels outraged at the needless vandalism perpetrated by an invader; Lakshmi has been smashed up and only a vestige is left, with the suggestion of a finger here, and an ornament there to indicate where Lakshmi sat. The ground is strewn with fingers, legs, and pieces of Narasimha, whose nose is broken off. The authors of these carvings, both the kings who thought of them and the sculptors who executed, were immortals, their conceptions godly in proportion.

Virupaksha temple is open and as ever built on a massive scale, which must have existed earlier than Vijayanagar. Its central hall was built by Krishnadevaraya to commemorate his coronation in 1509-10. The carvings and murals in the main hall are magnificent (though not the recent additions modelled in clay and coloured with garish enamel paint, which are incongruous). The gopuram in the courtyard is swarming with monkeys. Here in Hampi they are the rightful heirs to the land, if we go back to the days of Ramayana. This was the Kishkinda of the epic, which was ruled by Vali, who was the head of a race of monkeys, and where his brother Sugreeva was crowned by the grace of Rama later. Hampi has numerous associations with the

Ramayana. Rama, with his brother Lakshmana and Sita had camped near the Kodanda Rama Temple, before the abduction of Sita. When Sita was being carried off by Ravana she tied up her jewellery in a bundle and flung it down to indicate her route. It fell on a rock here, and was retrieved by Sugreeva, who kept it in a cave. A hill still called Anjanadari is said to be the birth place of Anjaneya. Sabara had her hermitage beside the Pampa lake. Matanga Hill, in which Sugreeva took refuge from Vali's wrath, lies to the east of Hampi.

Several accounts by ancient travellers—fortunately they have survived the Empire and its destroyers—give us an idea of the Vijayanagar capital. It was said to have been 64 square miles in extent. The Portuguese traveller Paes mentions that the city was as large as Rome, and the palace of the king was more spacious than the castles in Lisbon, but only the shattered remnants of its walls are to be seen now. One can let one's imagination roam over the old Bazaar Street in front of Virupaksha Temple, and arcades where flowers and gems, silk and ivory were heaped up and sold, and the sound of laughter and music filled the air, as men and beautiful women (a section of the city was named Soolay Street or the Street of Courtesans), pleasure-seekers, poets, artists, scholars and philosophers, jostled along, in their palanquins, on horses or on foot, and the bells of the elephants in their stables tinkled all day long. It was a civilization that had lasted three hundred years without a break.

CHITRADURGA

If one's destination is Bangalore on the completion of the journey through the 'Rockies', one has necessarily to pass through Chitradurga and Tumkur.

Under the Vijayanagar kings in the fifteenth century, there were vassal chieftains who held large tracts of the country and had their own armies. The most distinguished among them were the chiefs of Chitradurga and Nidugal.

The Chitradurga Nayaks were of Beda caste, hunters and mountaineers. All that we are able to gather of their early beginnings is that three families emigrated from somewhere near Tirupathi and settled in Bharmasagar. The grandson of one of these was the famous Thimmanna Nayak who was appointed in 1508 by the Vijayanagar king as Nayak of Holalkere and later of Chitradurga. He fortified the hill and surrounded himself with all the vestments of an independent ruler. Roused by this the Vijayanagar king despatched an army against him. During the siege the Nayak slipped out of his fort at dead of night and stole into the enemy's camp, planning to ride off on the horse belonging to the prince of Vijayanagar, who was commanding the army. As the Nayak was about to lift the rope off the peg to which it had been tied, the groom woke up. The horse thief flattened himself close to the earth and remained still. The groom drove the peg in once again, which went right through the hand of the Nayak's palm. He bore the pain, waited for the groom to fall asleep again, cut off the hand pegged to the ground, and made away with the horse.

Thimmanna Nayak's son. on the fall of Vijayanagar in 1564, assumed independence. In 1603, Kasturi Rangappa

Nayak succeeded him, and in his reign several battles were fought and Chitradurga territory was extended.

Fighting, annexing, losing, dying and reviving, the line continued. In 1762 Haidar Ali summoned the Nayak. The Nayak showed hesitation; Haidar's cavalry marched into the country and the Nayak was forced to pay a heavy fine and an annual tribute. Haidar attacked several times, whenever he found the Nayak's loyalty wavering or any delay in the payment of tribute. He finally annexed Chitradurga in 1779 and sent the Nayak and his family to Seringapatam as prisoners.

The Nidugal chiefs were another important line of rulers in this district, their territory extending from Chitradurga to Pavugada in Tumkur district and from Molakalmuru to Sira. The founder of the house was Tippanna Nayak, so named because he was picked as an infant from a dung-hill or rubbish heap. According to tradition his mother conceived by the Sun when she was only seven years old. Her father, considering it a disgrace to own the child, abandoned it on a dung-hill, from where it was picked up by a cowherd. A few years later the cowherd went to Kamalapur, near Vijayanagar, where there was an enclosure in which tigers were kept for show. One day, in the presence of the king, a tiger escaped and created a panic, but it was instantly killed by the boy who had come with the cowherd. The king grew interested in him and kept him in his court. Later the boy met and defeated a famous athlete who had been considered invincible. For all these exploits the king granted Tippanna a tract east of Chitradurga district, from where he extended his territory. He died in the latter half of the sixteenth century, and divided his territory among his seven sons, who relinquished their possessions when the Bijapur army invaded their territory.

Chitradurga town is at the foot of a rambling pile of rocky hills, with stretches of fort walls flanking the hills and often disappearing around a bend. A number of hills are scattered around, the top of each crowned with fort walls, with a central peak to be reached through winding pathways. Seven lines of fortifications are said to enclose the stronghold, but we cannot see the plan at one glance, since the walls have disappeared in some places, and indented with ranges of rock.

The palace in the inner fort was constructed by Tippu. Before it stands a gigantic trough, scooped out of a single stone and very well polished, which used to be filled with water for elephants to drink from. The upper hill fort has impressive fortifications, batteries, and masonry works, and several temples. Vestiges of the palace and fort of Palaygars are also there. The sturdy stone fortress, and the granaries as they now stand were built under Haidar's and Tippu's rule.

Five kilometers beyond the fort walls is situated the Murgi *math*, the residence of the chief *guru* of Lingayats. To the west, among a cluster of hills, is the *Ankli math*. Here are elaborate underground chambers, which are at least 400 years old. It is not possible to guess for what purpose these were built. The chambers were discovered with thick vegetation covering up the entrance, nearly a century ago when the *math* was established.

Nearby are also found, at Chandravalli, traces of an ancient city: and the Archaeological Department is engaged in reconstructing its period and history.

TUMKUR

Away from the main road, half an hour's journey takes one to a village called Gulur; a couple of furlongs' deviation from the village road, we arrive at a small grove in which nestles Kaidala village. At an ancient date it was the capital of a state and known as Kridapura. A comparatively recent and familiar association is the fact that it was the native village of Jakanachari, the famous sculptor. Nriparava was the ruler of Kridapura when Jakanachari began his career. His travels were extensive since he was engaged now at one court and now at another. At Belur, according to a vow, he cut off his arm, when an image he had been chiselling was proved to have a flaw.

The image was set aside as being unfit for worship. It was later found that the critic was none other than his son out in search of a long-lost father. After this Jakanachari was directed in a dream to return to his village and build a temple for Kesava. He obeyed the vision. When he completed the temple his arm was restored to him. *Kai Dala* means the restored arm. This temple can be seen even today. Some idea of its date is given by an inscription in the adjacent Iswara temple which was also built by Jakanachari. The inscription records that the temples were built in about 1150 in the reign of the Hoysala king, Narasimha.*

DEVARAYA DURGA

About 14 km from Tumkur, a fortified hill. Behind a forest bungalow at the foot of the hill there is a very attractive spot

---

* See Appendix 3 for full story.

called 'Namada Chilme'—a little cavity in a rocky bed, a cubit deep from which wells up an inexhaustible supply of water. This cavity, no bigger than a brass bowl, fills up as often as the water is removed, and supplies all the water needed for gardening, bathing, and washing, hereabouts. It is said that in the evenings peacocks, which are in plenty come out and dance around this spring. The place owes its name to the legend that Rama, while on his expedition to Lanka, camped at this spot. He needed water for mixing his *nama* (forehead marking), and created the spring with a touch of his finger.

The summit of Devaraya Durga is 1231 meters above sea level. The road winds up through thick jungles. On the summit is a temple dedicated to Narasimhaswami, and another temple for the same God, in the village, 245 meters below.

According to stories, a formidable robber chief had his stronghold here. He was subdued by Prince Sumati, son of a king of Karnata. After this enterprise he is said to have established a city near the present Nelamangala village in Bangalore district. There is also a tradition that on this hill there was a town called Anebiddajari, so named, because an elephant slipped and fell. An elephant, which was really a *Gandharva* in that form, suddenly appeared before the town and wrought havoc. For the people of the town there seemed to be no hope when the elephant itself saved the situation through its recklessness; it tried to rush up the steep rock on the west, fell back, and died.

In about 1696 Chikka Deva Raja of Mysore captured this hill from a chief of the name Jadaka and erected the fortifications, and the hill takes its name from him. His successor Kanteerava Raja built the temples.

MADDAGIRI

About 38 km from Tumkur, surrounded on all sides by hillocks and commanded by Maddagiri Durga, a fortified hill nearly 1230 meters high. The access is only from the northern face which slopes up so steeply that it is difficult to get a foot-hold on the bare slabs, except when the surface is perfectly dry. In times of war the garrison used to pour oil down the steep slabs and halt the advance of any attacking force.

The original fort and town were built by a local chief called Raja Hire Gowda. An interesting account is given of the founding of the town. A stray sheep returned from the hill dripping with water; this led to the discovery that there were plenty of springs on the hill, a town grew up in its vicinity, and mud fortifications were constructed on the hill for protection. In 1678, the descendants of the founder were defeated by the Raja of Mysore and the town was taken. The fortifications were improved by Haidar Ali. Tippu named it the City of Victory and made it the capital of the surrounding district. On the conclusion of the Third Mysore War, Maddagiri was included in Mysore territory.

SIRA

Another famous fortified town, about 53 km from Tumkur. The town was founded by Rangappa Nayak, the chief of Ratnagiri. Before the fort was completed, Sira and its dependencies were conquered by a Bijapur general, and then became a provincial capital of the Mughal Governors when Aurangzeb captured Bijapur in 1687. The last of the governors was Dilawar Khan, under whom this town attained great prosperity, and is said to have consisted of 50,000 houses. He built a very elegant palace, on the model of which the palaces of Seringapatam and Bangalore were later built. He also constructed a fine garden called Khan Bagh, which is believed to have suggested the model for the Lal Bagh of Bangalore.

Part Three

Whispers and Echoes

Of Bijapur district, a whole book would be justified, considering the wealth of history, relics, and monuments that it offers. Five rivers flow through the district,—Krishna, Bhima, Dhone, several streams joining the bigger rivers, Gataprabha and Malaprabha,—and yet the land looks as if drained of all moisture, highways without a shade, barren stony uplands, relieved curiously enough by tombs and ruins that stud the landscape,—in such abundance that curiosity ceases and one stops asking, 'What ruin is that?' or 'Whose tomb?'

Fortifications, bastions, domes and towers at the approach of Bijapur city. Six and a quarter miles of running walls, with a fifty-feet wide moat, wrap around the city; the walls are reinforced with several bastions, a running platform, and curtain-walls. Five mighty gates, at one time, controlled the entry into the town; the doors strengthened with spikes, bands, and clamps. Aurangzeb (as a prince and later as the Emperor at Delhi), who had made it his life's mission to subjugate Bijapur, succeeded only after twenty years of effort, and that too only by cutting off supplies of water and food to the beseiged forces.

The founder of Bijapur kingdom, Yusuf Adil Shah, was born in Constantinople in 1443, younger son of Aga Murad, Sultan of Constantinople. On the death of Murad, his successor ordered the destruction of his brother in accordance with the policy of leaving only a single male survivor for each generation. But the mother smuggled

Yusuf out of the country under the care of a Persian merchant, and Yusuf grew up in Persia. To avoid recognition, he fled from country to country and was finally destined to land at the port of Ratnagiri in 1461, when he had just turned seventeen. He possessed a commanding personality, and was versatile and accomplished. During a visit to Bidar, then the capital of Bahamani kingdom, he was sold to Mohamed Gawan, the minister; and by sheer excellence of character, he rose to great heights, earned the title of Adil Khan, and was appointed Governor of Bijapur. In 1489 he threw off his allegience to Bidar chiefs, and declared himself an independent ruler. Strangest pattern of a career—ranging from Constantinople to far-off Deccan. Adil Shah's dynasty, which held sovereignty for about 200 years (1489-1686), was brought to an end through the repeated, successive, attacks by Mugals, Maharattas, the British and finally Haidar and Tippu. The last of the Adil Shahi princes, Sikander, was only nineteen years old when produced before Emperor Aurangzeb, in silver chains. Aurangzeb stayed in Bijapur for two years after his victory. In 1689 plague broke out in his camp and his queen succumbed to it. Over a hundred thousand others perished. Bijapur became a city of death—the only activities therein being mourning and funerals, all normal business having come to a standstill. Even at that stage Aurangzeb refused to leave Bijapur, but obstinately held on. But when the princes in his camp fell sick one by one, he left. Following his exit, the fury of the epidemic abated, and in three years the city was completely free from it. The emperor returned, and strangely enough, ordered a census to be taken. The population which had been two million was now less than one million. It is not explained anywhere if Aurangzeb derived any satisfaction from this figure, and whether he viewed the pestilence as his ally or rival.

The achievements of the Bijapur rulers and their general culture have been testified in the records of Tavernier, Barbosa, and other foreign travellers. Its historical landmarks have really withstood the ravages of both Time and Battle. The list of important mosques and palaces, and tombs, in and around Bijapur city number over thirty. The outstanding ones are: Ibrahim Roza, the mausoleum of Ibrahim Adil Shah II and the mosque attached to it. Fergusson says of it: 'A group as rich and as picturesque as any in India, and far excelling anything of that sort on this side of Hellespont.'

The Dome of Gol Gumbuz looms over its surroundings, across at the other end conceived and constructed by Mohamed to rival Ibrahim Roza; it strikes an entirely different note in architecture. An enormous hall, square in shape, four lofty walls topped by octagonal towers at the corners, and surmounted by a gigantic dome without pillars. Standing on the gallery inside the dome, one experiences extraordinary acoustic effects—any whisper or the slightest rustling is amplified and echoed repeatedly, sound hitting and bouncing off wall to wall, amplifying and echoing again and again—truly symbolizing the history of this district.

Badami, Aihole and Pattadakal are places of importance in Bijapur district. Badami, 161 km from Bijapur city, was known as Vatapi and Badavi in the early inscriptions (sixth century AD). Badami was the capital of Chalukyas who ruled supreme from the sixth to the eighth century, whose conquests and expansions were remarkable in many ways. More than their conquests and historical importance, the

Chalukyan contributions to the development of arts and architecture are of lasting value; of the grandeur and sophistication of the kingdom under Chalukyas, we have an account of the empire by Hiuen Tsang, who travelled in India between 629 and 645 AD and visited the Chalukyan capital, at the time of Pulakesi II, the most famous among the Chalukyan rulers. Pulakesi II came to the throne at a time when his country was going through a period of internal confusion and external threats, which he warded off, and in course of time defeated the Kadambas, Gangas, Alopas, Cholas, Cheras, Pallavas and Pandyas, his greatest victory, however, being the overthrow of Harshavardhana of Kannauj. His empire extended from the Vindhyas to the Kaveri and from east coast to west coast. He proved such a wise and good sovereign, that his fame spread within the country and also outside. Hiuen Tsang included the Chalukya country in his itinerary, and has recorded that the Chalukyan kingdom was nearly 1930 km in 'circumference', and the capital was ten kilometres in 'circumference'. Of the people, he describes them as being tall and proud, sensitive and friendly, but vengeful when injured, and loyal to their king. Further he gives us a detailed account of the political, military, social and economic conditions, which indicates a very high degree of development in every field.

In 642, Pulakesi was defeated by the Pallava king, Narasimha Varma, in revenge for the former's attack on the Pallava capital earlier. From this point the Chalukyan eminence noticeably declined. In 757, the last of the dynasty, Kirtivarman II, was overthrown, and power passed on to the Rashtrakutas, during whose domination Chalukyas existed as stragglers, in a feudatory capacity, here and there. Among such stragglers was one Taila II, who was an officer under the Rashtrakuta king, and who seized an opportunity to re-establish the Chalukyan power, by putting to death the last of the Rashtrakutas; he declared himself the king at Malkhed at first, but later moved his capital to Kalyana in Bidar district (973-997). Again, after being eclipsed for nearly two centuries, the Chalukyan power revived and continued for about fifty years, when one Bijjala Kallachuri, a Commander of the army, exterminated the remnants of the Chalukyan family, and declared himself the ruler.

The noteworthy feature of his reign was the advent of Basaveswara, the founder of Lingayat sect. He was a minister under Bijjala, but had a rational and humanistic outlook; he denounced casteism, superstition, and reliance on meaningless rituals.

The lamb brought
to the sacrifice
chewed the green buntings at the door.
It sought to quench its hunger
Not knowing
its death.
Born a moment ago, died the next.
Did those who killed
Live,
Lord of Koodala Sangama?

They pour libations of milk
on a cobra carved in stone:
They say 'Kill!'
when they set their eyes upon a living snake.
They refuse the *jangama* who asks for food,

but offer a meal
To the Linga which does not eat.*

He proclaimed his faith and propagated his outlook (mostly through 'Vachanas') and attracted a large following. Lingayat faith became as prominent as any other major religious movement such as Vaishnavism, Jainism and Orthodox Saivaism. When political and theological differences arose with Bijjala, Basaveswara thought it would be best to leave Kalyan, and retreated to the serene atmosphere of Kudala Sangama at the confluence of Krishna and Malaprabha and spent his later days there.

Badami, Pattadakal and Aihole form a group, and display the achievements of Chalukyan architecture; all three are close to each other within a radius of fifty kilometers.

Badami is situated at the mouth of a ravine between two ranges of rocky hills, which remind one of Arizona in the US—horizontal strata of rocks piled one upon another, loom over this ancient state capital, which is now a little village. The hillside has been excavated and the temples built. While they could have built them with less labour on the plains, they chose to hew the rocks to house the gods in caves, and provide them thus, an indestructible shelter. Racially those that raised these temples must have been hardier, beyond our concept. The very manual labour involved in tackling this mass and shaping them appears superhuman. The very steps hewn to take us over to the site seem forbidding and one hesitates to put one's foot on them.

---

* Translated by M. Shankar.

Part Four

Bangalore and Mysore

BANGALORE

A hunter was separated from his companions. Night came on suddenly. He sighted a small hut, and knocked on the door; an old woman came out.

'I have lost my way, mother, give me some food.'

'You look a noble man, Sir, and what should I have fit for you to eat?'

'Anything. I am hungry.'

'I have a bean-field behind my house and it has yielded me a good crop this year. If your taste permits it . . .' Presently she placed a plateful of beans before the visitor, and he ate it with great relish, found grass for his horse too, and was on his way again.

It was later learnt that this visitor was none other than the king himself, and the village came to be known as the Town of Boiled Beans (Bendha Kaluru later abbreviated to 'Bangaluru').

When we emerge from the mists of tradition, we learn that Kempe Gowda I built the town in 1537 AD and constructed a mud fort around it. Sensing that this town was bound to grow beyond the walls of his mud fort, he built watch-towers at four points to indicate its future boundaries. On the North at Bellary Road, South at Lal Bagh, the Eastern one on a rock near Ulsoor, the Western overlooking Kempambudi Tank.

An astrologer studied the conjunction of stars and fixed an auspicious day on which Kempe Gowda marked off, with the sharp end of a plough, two streets, one running east to west (between Ulsoor Gate and Railway Goods shed) and the other running north to south (from Yelahanka Gate to the fort). Thereafter he built temples for Vinayaka who brings luck, and Anjaneya, the God of Power. He also built the famous Bull Temple (Basavangudi), and many others.

The astrologer had displayed great astuteness and foresight. The area within the markings of the plough, now throbs with life and activity (even too much of it as it may seem), if one watches the flow of traffic and the jam of pedestrians in the streets running east to west, and north to south, intersecting, cutting, weaving themselves into a bewildering maze of main streets, proliferating into side-streets, lanes, bylanes, and blind alleys, without a square inch of space being left unused.

The octogenarian one notices on a pyol, spiritedly arguing with a circle of cronies, must have learnt or taught the alphabet in that children's school under a faded sign-board, those pawn-brokers seated cross-legged, in their narrow parlours, amidst a heap of used clothes and metal-ware, probably have been philosophers and guides to desperate souls seeking ready cash. And ranged along further, yarn-brokers, cycle-repairers, and grain merchants; vendors of sweets displaying seductively a hundred delicacies on trays, all these must have come of a long line of octogenarians, sweet-vendors, pawnbrokers, and the rest, forming the warp and weft of the social fabric hereabout.

Passing down, one may also have a sudden glimpse of the face of a god, shining in the soft light of a wick-lamp inside a shrine, of devotees kneeling in silent prayer inside a mosque, and a church too, where I step in to read the inscription under a portrait in the foyer: 'Rev. Benjamin Rice (1814-1887)—an unwearisome labourer in various departments. An excellent Kanarese Preacher, who delivered his sermons in Kannada for over fifty years.' That was in 1830 or thereabouts. The loungers, one notices, reclining on the rusty shutters of a closed shop also have a look of permanence about them. Everything and everyone here bears an institutional touch, giving one a feeling that they must have gone on living here generation after generation, never stepping beyond their teeming orbit, and may not have even noticed the development of Bangalore in other directions. Sadashivanagar, Jayanagar and Raj Mahal Extension may sound alien to their ears, accustomed as they are to 'Nagarathpet', 'Tharagupet', 'Chickpet', and 'Doddapet'.

This hoary nucleus of the city retains an indescribable charm, although the architecture may look outdated, and one's passage at first may appear hazardous through its traffic, but actually the wheels steer off within a hair's breadth and spare the pedestrian's toes, who must survive by lightly leaping aside, and recovering his balance from the very edge of the granite pavement, and may not suffer more than an occasional jab from a cycle handle or a bump from its mudguard as crack-riders dash past, weaving their way through. Here the shops may look unsophisticated, being mostly without glossy counters, glazed windows, or furniture, except a desk for the proprietor at the entrance, but you could get anything and everything you may desire within this ancient perimeter (crowned by the magnificent Krishnarajendra Market), if you stand on the threshold, catch someone's eyes and make your demands clearly heard over other people's demands and general conversation. Anything and everything including a full regalia with sparkling crown and robes for an emperor in a court scene for a theatrical production, and also false hair, beards, lace-caps, and masks. A whole row of them I had seen some years ago, although on a recent visit, I could not locate those shops, as they seemed to have got hemmed between watch-repairs and automobile spares and tinkers.

*

Founder Kempe Gowda's vision has been fulfilled and exceeded. One has only to go up the Corporation Multi-Storey twenty-fourth floor to appreciate the vastness of Bangalore spreading out in every direction for 130 square kilometers. I was overwhelmed with its extent again, during a drive through the city with the Corporation Administrator, Mr Laxman Rao (who leaves home at the dawn of each day to inspect this vast city methodically inch by inch and pass orders on the spot to his staff accompanying him, dedicated as he is, to the task of maintaining Bangalore as a city of beauty and comfort—'It is like house-keeping, you have to be at it continuously,' he remarked), from Jayanagar Shopping Complex (the biggest of its kind in Asia, with its 225 shops, super bazars, fruit and vegetables market, offices and a cinema-theatre) at one end, to Ulsoor Tank at the other. Parks and mini-forests, that are being created and cherished all along the way seemed countless. Eliminating congestion by demolition and widening of roads, construction of pavements, garbage removal through slow-moving trolleys into which people are encouraged to throw all waste and rubbish, and building of a huge wholesale market at Kalaspalayam to draw away the concentration of lorries and men at Krishnarajendra Market, are major plans that are being executed without respite or a pause.

A section of the city where you can hear statements such as: 'Winston Churchill lived here', or 'We were suppliers of cigars to Churchill', or 'Duke of Wellington's descendants have always ordered their shoes from us. They are still sending us Christmas greetings.' One can hear such claims in and around Commercial Street or Brigade Road or Russel Market, which prospered in the days when this part of the city was very much anglicized, being occupied by British or Anglo-Indian officials and military personnel.

This part of the city enjoyed a topographical caste superiority at one time, being a 'Cantonment' area distinct from the 'City', which was 'Native'. Even today certain streets and areas retain their British associations, such as Richmond Town, Cox Town, Lavalle Road, Fraser Town, St Marks, Kensington, Johnson Market and so forth. I fervently hope that some zealot will not think of changing them but appreciate their historical flavour;—at least to honour the memory of men and women who set forth from far off Britain in those days with dreams of a flourishing career in the 'Orient' and sadly enough, laid their bones in Bangalore soil. I visited an old cemetery in the Cantonment, in order to look for the grave of a soldier, who was court-martialled and shot for indiscipline, the said act of indiscipline being nothing more than quaffing a glass of water, while the Commandant had ordered the company to drink only beer. The soldier had no taste for beer (or any alcohol) and had to face death-penalty for it. In that forest of tomb-stones, overgrown with weeds and thicket, I could not find this particular grave of one who was forbidden to drink water, perhaps, as a protection against cholera, but could not escape death anyway. The inscriptions over the tombs have a harrowing tale to tell of men, women and children, who could not survive the Indian climate or conditions of those days, and seemed to have come thousands of miles only to die. In addition to Smiths and Ogilvys, Captains, Lieutenants, or Corporals, dead in their thirties, their wives passed away mostly in their twenties or even less and the children never lived beyond ten, and infants aged a few days. In the early eighteenth century, before the discovery of inoculations and antibiotics, when pneumonia, dysentery or malaria struck, there could be no hope of survival. I noticed in a whole row, an entire family wiped out by cholera.

*

In and around Bangalore are located industrial establishments of the first magnitude. Hindustan Aeronautics, New Electric Government Factory, Soap Factory, Hindustan Machine Tools, Bharat Electronics, Indian Telephone Industries, to mention only a few, each one employing several thousand workers, handling a variety of sophisticated, up-to-date machinery. To list them all would cover several pages. On the road to Whitefield alone are situated a hundred odd major factories. The Industrial Estate at Rajajinagar at the other end of the city has hundreds of small-scale and ancillary units—with a well-ordered 'Tool Room' to help in designing machine tools for any special purpose.

Bangalore has been essentially a centre of scientific, technological and research activities. The old palace of the Maharaja, I learn, is to be converted into a Museum of Living Science, which will concentrate in one place, exhibits of permanent value for experts and students alike.

Sir M. Visvesvaraya whose vision and practical genius gave shape to modern Karnataka in its civic, industrial, and engineering fields, lived and died in Bangalore, a centenarian, active to the last in the pursuit of his ideal of modernizing Karnataka. The Industrial Museum at the Cubbon Park stands as a tribute to the memory of this rare and unique personality.

Living in Bangalore, no one can complain of a dull moment. There are nearly a hundred cinema theatres, the largest concentration perhaps, for any place, regular theatrical productions at Rabindra Kalakshetra, or in the professional repertory theatres. Sporting events, racing, classical concerts or jazz and pop music, not to speak of seminars, conferences, art and religious festivals, attract an enormous influx of visitors by road, train and plane. It is estimated that at any time a floating population of five lakhs, could be counted in Bangalore, a city so cosmopolitan in character, that all languages of India could be heard there, if one is inclined to go on a linguistic hunt. Bangalore is connected to the very ends of the earth by air, road and rail and that seems to me one of the finest advantages of life in Bangalore. I have discussed the subject of Bangalore with persons in other parts of India, and have found that ninety out of hundred dream of settling down in Bangalore, after retirement, and a few have already, with foresight, built houses, and are preoccupied with the strategy to get their houses back from the tenants now occupying them. For youth and middle age, life in Bangalore offers many attractions. For the aged, Bangalore air has proved salubrious. There are more pensioners settled in Bangalore than in another part of India. Many an old guard, in different walks of life, well-known names, might be out of view for decades and presumed to have left the world, but one will have an agreeable surprise coming upon the venerable gentleman at a City club playing bridge, or strolling quietly along the garden paths of Lal Bagh or the pavement of Whitefield, or occupying an unobtrusive seat at the Gayana Samaj concerts. Bangalore is actually a walker's paradise: in spite of its crowds and traffic and buildings, it still provides a hundred places where one can walk in peace according to one's choice, Cubbon Park right across the city, Vidhana Soudha terrace gardens, Lal Bagh, around Gold Course or Sankey Tank, not to mention the promenades in a crowded shopping area such as Mahatma Gandhi Road or Narasimha Raja Road.

There are many attractive places within a thirty to sixty kilometers range of the city—Nandi Hills, Hesarghatta, and Mekedatu. Bannerghatta, within an hour's drive of Bangalore, would, however, be my first choice for a weekend. Bannerghatta is now being developed as a National Park, without in any way spoiling its mountainous and jungle characteristics, which possess a rugged charm. A safari area is being created where one will be able to move on an equal tooting with lions in a free state. Besides the larger wildlife, birds (one hundred kinds of birds have been observed), monkeys, bison, and elephants, panther, wild boar, sambar, spotted deer, jackal, Indian hare, barking deer, hog deer, and sloth bear will tenant this Park without being cramped in captivity.

Another place I would recommend is Thippagondana Halli, where river Arkavathi is impounded for supplying water to Bangalore. About 32 km away from Bangalore—the range of hills around, and the water-spread, afford an inspiring scene, especially when the birds dive in the lake, with the evening sun sliding behind the hills.

MYSORE

When in Bangalore, I generally feel a regret that I didn't make it my home (instead of Mysore), considering the advantages—its cosmopolitan air, amenities, accessibility to any part of the world, climate, and all the excellences of urban life. But actually Mysore has been my home—for half a century now. It just happened that way, that's all; and every time I go back to Mysore, I feel thankful to Heavens for placing me there. The very approach by road or train, crossing the Kaveri bridge, with the Chamundi Hill coming on view, is delightful as one passes through rolling meadows and paddy fields, and with the sky-line unpunctuated by factory chimneys (yet, although an industrial belt is fast developing along Hunsur and Krishnarajasagar Roads).

Mysore has been classified technically as a 'backward' area, and inducements are being offered for the starting of industries, so as to bring it up to modern standards, freed from the background of a traditional agricultural economy that dominated it for centuries. The patronage of the Palace was also there, keeping alive art and culture, and several elegant professions such as those of perfumers, ivory or sandalwood carvers, and florists.

Mysore Mallige is considered the jasmine of Jasmines, which blooms in April-May, charging the air with fragrance not only in the gardens, but also from the trays and baskets of hawkers, at the market, while women keenly examine the white full buds and argue over the price before taking them home. Photographers have a busy season now as little girls love to have their hair braided with jasmine buds and photograph themselves from many angles. This rich harvest comes just in time for the Ramanavami, the festival celebrating Rama's incarnation on earth. For ten days: every corner of the city will resound with music, concerts being held in halls or blocked-off street corners, with maestros from far and near singing or playing their instruments, to a vast, appreciative audience. An image or picture of Rama festooned with flowers set up on the dais, presides over the function, which, commencing early in the evening, may go on until midnight. Admission to the concerts will be mostly free and unrestricted, the expenses being met by voluntary contributions, and 'Plate Collection'. Each day's programme will conclude with a *pooja* and distribution of *prasada*, a little packet of sugar, coconut, and sliced banana in a rare amalgam. Some uneasiness is likely to be felt by the organizers at some stage in the proceedings, as the 'Rain-God' may also attempt to participate in the festivities. Evening Rains (which is a mild and misleading term for the grand opera of the Heavens, which may all of a sudden open with thunder, lightning, and stormy winds tearing up lamp posts, electric wires, pandal roofs, paralysing traffic with flooded roads), is an anticipated event in this season, as life in Mysore is regulated by South-West Monsoon (*Mungara* as it is known), which cools the summer heat (between March and

June). But the organizers anxiously watch the hill for the dark clouds gathering on its summit in the evening, and pray that rains may hold off . However, Ramanavami goes on undaunted, and concludes on the tenth day with pipe and drum and a grand procession of the deity taken out in an illuminated chariot.

Mysoreans cherish their festivals: Yugadi, Ramanavami, Deepavali and Dasara. On the eve of every festival, you will find Sayyaji Rao Road and the city-market gates impenetrable. Money and economic motives seem to recede in the background at such times, as all work slows down a day before, ceases for a couple of days, and makes a tardy start all over again as the festive hang-over lingers. The festive temperament is more marked in Mysore than anywhere else. Any industrialist who starts an enterprise in Mysore has to reckon on this psychology, if he is not to despair later. But no damage is actually done as work, somehow, is resumed and goes on everywhere, factories turn out their products, house-building activities continue, and plumbers and electricians attend to the repairs sooner or later.

To equate Mysore with an industrial city, such as Bangalore, would be inapt. Those totally dedicated to Bangalore life, find it hard to spend more than a day in Mysore. After a tourist round of visits to the zoo, the temple on the Chamundi Hill, the Palace, Bird Sanctuary, Tippu's fort, and the Sandal Oil and Silk Factories, and an evening spent amidst the colourful fountains of Brindavan, they feel that their business is over, and they have nothing further to do as the city has to offer, normally, nothing more by way of entertainment or engagement. However, there are also certain seasons of first-class sporting events, such as football, cricket, basketball, and so on which attract the youth. But the largest draw is often wrestling bouts in Doddakere, watched by milling crowds at week-end. Mysore still maintains in every part of the city its 'Garadi', with red-striped walls, within which are located wrestling clubs, which maintain the orthodox wrestling traditions, and draw out in challenge champions from all parts of the country—Punjab down to Cape Comorin.

The quality of life that Mysore offers is unique. The atmosphere is placid and poetic, and one is constantly tempted to enjoy the moment setting aside all other thoughts. Not only the festivals but certain seasons of pilgrimages are compulsive. Mysore city's original nucleus has been a number of villages—the three *Koppals*, Padavarhalli, Kesare, and Asokapuram, which supply the bulk of workers for our factories, fields, gardens and public works, and also artisans, and mechanics. But these are the very ones to be seen marching down the street on a pilgrimage to Mahadeswara Hills during Sivarathri and Yugadi, a trip of over one hundred miles to and fro, each member carrying a bamboo staff, ready to walk through dense forests, with faith at heart and no kind of fear, the air echoing with shouts of 'Jai' to the God they are out to visit.

Mysore offers certain special delicacies for the connoisseur in food. The 'Nanjangud Plantain' with a flavour unknown to other varieties—there are enthusiasts who would go miles to attain the 'Nanjangud', tiny, golden, rather hard-looking but absolutely ambrosial to the taste; this particular brand is gradually vanishing before the commercially cultivated imitation, but still there are one or two places known only to the expert, where it is available—a small corner shop in Old Agrahar, from whose ceiling bunches of 'Nanjangud' hang, where you just ask for it and not stoop to discuss the price, and it will be packed up for you with the advice, 'Keep it for a day and then eat', and you depart without further ado: and then a shop at the city market, where you should not ask. 'Is this the real "Nanjangud"?'—because he won't keep it otherwise. And then follow the master if you like to find other delicacies such as Hurigalu (spiced, parched gram), Kobri Mittai, Masala Dosai and 'Set Dosa' (the last served only in sets of four with Chutney)—these may not be immediately available anywhere and everywhere, but under expert guidance, one can attain them in modest-looking eating corners. Not to mention the fruits in each season. and the *Avaraikalu* (a bean variety), which retains its special flavour when plucked in winter mist, and so drives some connoisseurs to leave their bed for the field where it is cultivated, at pre-dawn hours. Or Soppina Kadale Kai—tender Bengal gram in bunches, with roots and leaves intact; you accept it like a bouquet from the vendor and pluck the tender pod, and pop it into your mouth while walking or in the intervals of talking. Soppina Kadale, however, comes closely on the heels of Avaraikalu. When the village-carts come rumbling into the streets laden with the Soppu, the expert will read the sign and declare immediately: 'Avaraikalu is over—what'll be left in the market will be hard and over-priced!'

It is not all festivals and fine weather, and special food. Mysore has a background of academic life—it is essentially a University town. Oriental Research Institute containing rare books and manuscripts, the colleges of engineering, medicine, Ayurveda, and Sanskrit, besides the arts colleges spread over the city, have a student population of over

20,000. Manasa Gangotri—a name coined by the poet K. V. Puttappa—at the western end of the city on a ground of 300 acres, with its own buildings, and hostels and other amenities, is a world by itself, where postgraduate studies in science, humanities and commerce, and research in Kannada language and literature, are pursued.

*

Here is an extract from my memoirs, which will convey an idea of Mysore's possibilities:

> . . . I found the classroom windows revealing trees and birds, or meadows with cows placidly chewing grass and perhaps the cowherd sitting in the shade. In such a setting, I found the teacher's voice a meaningless drone, which one had to tolerate perforce. From the eastern corridors of the Maharaja's College, one saw the Chamundi Hill in all its fullness framed in arches along the parapet; Maharaja's College was on one ridge of the city, with the hill and the Lalitha Mahal Palace on the other; in the valley in between lay the city with the golden dome of the palace standing out. During the political-science hour, one could watch the shadow of clouds skimming the mountainside, alternating with patches of sunlight, or the mirage shimmering across the landscape, and nothing seemed more irrelevant than the lecturer's voice falling on our ears. . . .
>
> . . . there was also a glimpse of the Oriental Library, with friezes depicting the life of God Krishna along its walls and inscribed pillars on its lawns, where once again one noticed cows grazing with concentration and contentment. During my college years, I became so

familiar with the scenic details and their transformations around that I could have drawn up, if need be, a time-table of the natural events. During June and July, for instance, fitful drizzling alternated with sunlight bursting through the clouds, and a rainbow, sometimes arched over the hill. If a painter had attempted to put all these things on his canvas, he would have been berated for overstatement, but Nature, having no such qualms about criticism, was exuberant and profuse and distracted my attention from my lessons.

. . . Every morning I left for a walk around Kukanahalli Tank, with a book in my pocket. It could be Palgrave's *Golden Treasury*, or Tagore's *Gitanjali*, or Keats in the World's Classics. After a walk around the tank, I sat down under a lone tree on a rise of the ground, opened the book, and partially read and partially observed the water birds diving in. Of course cows and goats, ubiquitous in Mysore, grazed around. But everything fitted into the scheme beautifully. I read until noon and started back home. Sometimes I went back to the Kukanahalli Tank in the late afternoon, when the evening sun touched the rippling water-surface to produce uncanny lighting effects, and the western sky presented a gorgeous display of colours and cloud formations at sunset. Even today, I would assert, after having visited many parts of the world, that nowhere can you witness such masterpiece of sunsets as in Mysore. I would sit on a bench on the tank and watch the sun's performance, the gradual fading of the colours in the sky, and the emergence of the first single star at dusk. When the monsoon broke, one could watch dark mountainous clouds mustering, edged with lightning; these would develop awesome pyrotechnics. In June, drizzle and sunshine alternating, leaving Gold Mohur,

Flame of the Forests, and Jacaranda in bloom along the avenues. In July and August, the neverending downpour, greyladen skies, and the damp air blowing. I was fascinated by all the seasonal changes. Tagore's poetry (although I may be somewhat more critical today) swept me off my feet in those days. When I read:

> *'In the deep shadows of the rainy July,*
> *with secret steps, thou walkest'*

I felt I was inducted into the secrets of Nature's Glory. I enjoyed every moment of living in Mysore. Sometimes I loitered through the parks and the illuminated vicinities of the Maharaja's Palace. Some days I climbed the thousand steps of the hill and prayed at the shrine of Chamundi, made coconut offerings, and ate them with great relish on the way back. Some days I would notice the gathering storm and flee before it, running down the thousand steps and a couple of miles from the foot of the hill, to reach home drenched, dripping and panting, but feeling victorious at having survived the blinding lightning and thunder. Chamundi Hill offered not only a temple to visit, but also uncharted slopes, boulders, creeks and unsuspected retreats. Our exploration once brought us to a cave-temple with pillared platforms, secret chambers, and underground cellars, the entire structure roofed over by a huge rock, at the southern base of Chamundi Hill. I took to visiting this cave regularly, not caring for the rumour that the place might be harbouring reptiles and cheetahs in its cellars.

Part Five

Here and There

A BATTLE-FIELD

About 14 km from Mysore the great river Kaveri divides into two branches which meet again about five kilometers further down; and these parted arms enclose a space of land known as Seringapatam. This island was covered with jungles when Sage Gautama came and settled here a few thousand years ago. In 894 AD, a person named Tirumalaiya built a temple for Ranganatha and called the place Sri Ranga Pura. Nearly three centuries later it became one of the eight townships on the banks of Kaveri assigned by Vishnuvardhana to his guru Ramanujacharya. Still three centuries later one Timmanna visited Vijayanagar and obtained permission to build a fort around the island. He had discovered a hidden treasure and he used it for constructing the fort; he also improved the temple of Ranganatha with the stone and materials he had secured from the destruction of 101 Jain temples in a nearby town.

A temple, a fort, and a town coming up—these developments were noticed by prying eyes. The island left alone for so many centuries to its river-washed existence now briskly changed hands in less than half a century. An old inscription tells us that Narasa, founder of the second Vijayanagar dynasty, 'Quickly damming up the Kaveri when in full flood, crossed over and captured the enemy alive in a battle. Taking possession of their kingdom, he made the ancient Srirangapatna his own.' Thus begun, the noise of battle rolled on for well over four hundred years, around this unhappy island. First under the rule of the Viceroys of Vijayanagar and then under Raja Wodeyar, the rising ruler of Mysore. Following an engagement at Talakad, which ended in the death of the Viceroy, and of his wife, Raja Wodeyar made Seringapatam his capital. In 1638 it was besieged by the Bijapur forces, which Kantirava Narasaraj repulsed: later Sivappa Nayak of Bednur besieged it; nearly at the end of the century the Maharattas attacked it; in 1732 the Nawab of Arcot sent a powerful army against Seringapatam; in 1735 the Subedar of Deccan marched on it aided by a French force, and peace was purchased for 56 lakhs. 'The treasury being empty, one-third was raised on the plate and jewels of the Hindu temples and the property and ornaments of the Raja, and for the remainder bills were given, which, however, were never redeemed.' In 1757 and 1759 the Maharattas attacked the island; during this second visit, the defence was entirely in the hands of Haidar Ali, a cavalryman at one time, now risen to high command by sheer merit. After this, the most memorable sieges were by the British in 1792 and 1799 in the reign of Tippu Sultan.

In 1792 the attack was led by Lord Cornwallis. On the 5th of February he encamped within a short distance of Seringapatam. The Sultan strengthened his defences and encamped on the north bank of the river. At about eight o'clock on the 6th, with the moonlight on the flowing Kaveri, the British force, formed into three columns, marched on in dead silence: the centre column being under the command of Cornwallis himself. This was rather a surprise to Tippu, who thought that Lord Cornwallis would wait for the arrival on the south, of General

Abercromby's army which was then at Periyapatna. At about eleven o'clock the head of the centre column was spotted by the advance cavalry of Tippu. When the column reached the edge of the north bank it was received with heavy fire, but it pressed on, making its way through bayonet-charge and gained the south bank; another party followed and occupied the suburb on the east, Shahar Ganjam. By about 1 p.m., various other companies pressed on and occupied positions of vantage in different parts of the island. On the 16th, Abercromby's army and a Maharatta contingent arrived and joined the British force.

On the 24th, allied troops, waiting to take the fort, received intimation that negotiations for peace were going on and that all trench work was to be stopped forthwith. Tippu was given the following terms of peace: he was to give up half the dominions he possessed before the war, pay an indemnity of three crores and thirty lakhs of rupees, release all the prisoners held since the time of his father, and deliver two of his sons as hostages to the British.

The scene on the 26th harrowed all the onlookers. The two sons, aged eight and ten, were being delivered as hostages. The fort walls were crowded with soldiers and citizens, who watched in utter silence and dismay as the caparisoned elephants bearing the hostages neared the gateway. Tippu himself stood on the bastion above the main entrance and watched his sons go.

As the elephants emerged from the fort-gate, a salute of guns was fired by the artillery at Seringapatam, and as they approached the British lines, a salute was fired there too. They were met half way and conducted under a guard of honour. The procession was a gorgeous one led by camels and seven standard bearers and followed by a hundred pikemen carrying silver-inlaid spears. The princes were received by the troops presenting arms and officers saluting. Lord Cornwallis received them at the entrance to his tent with an embrace. Gulam Ali, who had to conduct the actual surrendering of the hostages said: 'These children were till this morning the sons of my master. Their situation is now changed and they must look up to your lordship as their father.'

We get an idea of Seringapatam of this time from a description given by one Major Dirom, who was an officer in the army: 'This pettah or town of modern structure built on the middle and highest part of the island, is about half a mile square, divided into regular cross streets, all wide, shaded on each side by trees and full of good houses, for the accommodation of the bazaar people and merchants and for the convenience of troops stationed in that part of the island for its defence. A little way to the eastward of the pettah is the entrance into the great garden of Lal Bagh, which occupies the east end of the island, possessing all the beauty and convenience of a country retirement, is dignified by the mausoleum of Haidar, and a superb new palace built by Tippu. To these add the idea of an extensive suburb or town, which filled the middle space between the fort and the garden full of wealthy industrious inhabitants, and it will be readily allowed that this insulated metropolis must have been the richest, most convenient and beautiful spot possessed in the present age by any native prince in India.'

The siege of 1799 was under the command of General Harris. Tippu in the interval between the previous siege and this had greatly strengthened the fortifications. General Harris arrived at Seringapatam on the 5th of April after defeating Tippu at Malavalli, a nearby village. In the improved defence scheme there was a new line of entrenchment on the south of the fort from the Daulat Bagh to Periyapatna bridge, about seven hundred yards from the fort, and Tippu's infantry were placed between these works and the river.

General Stuart joined the main army on the 14th. The regular siege commenced from the 17th. The first attack was to be at the western angle across the river.

On the 27th the Mysore army was driven from the last boundary of outer defence. On the morning of 2nd May the guns on the British side kept a continuous fire, and formed a breach, and had greatly enlarged it by the evening. 1 p.m. on the 4th was fixed for the assault under the command of General Baird with a body of troops numbering 4,376. Before daybreak they had taken their stand in the trenches with scaling ladders and other equipment. At one o'clock precisely Baird stepped forward from the trenches in full view of both the armies, flourishing his sword, calling upon his men to follow him. In less than seven minutes the British flag was planted on the summit of the breach.

Since the siege began Tippu had been living in a small tent on the southern part of the fort directing the operations. When the enemy batteries were firing, he moved from this exposed position to an apartment formed by an old gateway leading to the river on the north. The troops on duty inside the fort numbered 13,750. He had assigned the general charge of the angle attacked to Sayyed Sahib, his father-in-law, who was to be assisted by Sayyed Gaffur, who had formerly been an officer in the British service. The Sultan's son with the whole of the cavalry assisted by Purnaiya was detailed to parry the northern attack, encamping at Karighatta. His second son commanded the Mysore Gate on the southern side of the fort. His most trusted, and dependable commander of the light cavalry, Kamruddin, with a body of 4,000 troops, was out to disrupt the flow of supplies and reinforcements to the enemy.

On the morning of the 4th, Sayyed Gaffur came to the Sultan to say that he detected feverish activity in the British lines and that an assault might be coming any moment now. Tippu didn't think anybody would dare to advance during the day. At about nine o'clock Tippu proceeded to his palace, bathed and gave alms to mendicants. He returned to his gateway apartment at about midday and had just begun his lunch when he heard that the assault had commenced and that Sayyed Gaffur was the foremost casualty. 'Sayyed Gaffur was never afraid to die,' he commented, and ordered another officer to take his place. He abandoned his food, and hurried towards the breach, along the northern rampart. Standing within two hundred yards of the breach, he fired at his assailants, with his own hands. Seeing that most of his men were lying dead or wounded and that the attackers were pressing on, he retired along the rampart. He was also slightly wounded. At this juncture he found his horse near at hand, mounted it, and proceeded towards a gateway leading to the inner fortress when he got mixed up with a panic-stricken and fleeing crowd of soldiers and citizens who were trying to reach the river and ford it. The assailants poured in fire here. Tippu's horse fell dead, and he received a wound in the chest, and was half fainting when his attendants reached him and placed him on a palanquin. The dead and the wounded lay around in mounds, with their clothes catching fire from the paper of the cartridges. The Sultan's palanquin was kept near an archway, as it could not be carried through. He was trying to wriggle out of it helplessly, when a British soldier attracted by the jewelled sword belt of the Sultan, tried to snatch it, but the Sultan seized his sword and with a final effort slashed his leg; whereupon the soldier raised his musket and shot him through the temple.

Hours later a search was made for Tippu's body. By the glimmering light of a torch it was found late at night (over 11,000 bodies were found floating in the moats and under the debris): an amulet was tied round his arm; and a tiny copy of Koran in a silver case, the crimson cloth round his waist, and his pouch with red-and-green tassel, helped in identifying his body, which was taken to the palace the next day and buried with military honours beside his father's at Lal Bagh.

*

Srirangapattana is a battle-scarred town, with memorable landscapes. Here in front of the railway which cuts through the western portion of the fort, are the Garrison Hospital, and the Breach, with a simple monument over it, and there the dungeon in which many a prisoner of war spent his dismal hours; and the grass-covered piece of ground shows us where Tippu's palace once stood. Beyond it the Water Gate where he had his camp during the siege, and that fenced-off piece of ground further up is the spot where he fell. Outside the fort is the Daria Daulat, the summer palace set in an exquisite garden on the river bank, built in 1784 by Tippu. At the eastern end of the island is the Gumbaz where Tippu lies with his parents. On the south of the Daria

Daulat is a small monument to the memory of the fallen officers in the final siege; and then the Garrison Cemetery opened in 1800, where lies many a soldier. Here we see a tombstone on which is inscribed the name of Mrs Scott. She was the wife of Colonel Scott who was in charge of a gun factory in Ganjam, and they lived with their child in a bungalow, built for them by the Maharaja. One April morning, Colonel Scott left for French Rocks on inspection duty, and when he returned, he found his wife and child dead, succumbing to a sudden attack of cholera, and their bodies were laid out on their bed. On seeing it Colonel Scott drowned himself in the Kaveri, which flows through his garden. People believed, at one time, that Colonel Scott comes up from the river at right and joins his wife and child in the bungalow. It looks, no doubt, haunted. Someone seems to have successfully exorcized the ghosts and now lives happily in this enchanting bungalow on the river.

The whole island has a haunted appearance, with its countless monuments, tombs, and cemeteries; and with its bungalows and palaces tenanted only by caretakers or guides, where once must have resided some distinguished soldier, sultan or administrator.

TALAKAD

An ancient city on the left bank of Kaveri, about 45 km from Mysore. The actual site of the old city is now under sand, stretching for nearly a mile; the sand billows crept on the town at the rate of nine or ten feet a year and before it the population retreated inland, and a new town is now in existence. The buried town is of great antiquity. More than

thirty temples are under sand; the most important of them
is Kirtinarayana's which is occasionally opened up with
great difficulty during certain festivals. Only the tower over
the inner shrine and the front portal are visible above the
sand. It is a magnificent temple in.Hoysala style. The deity
of the temple, Narayana, is eight feet in height and stands
on a pedestal. The outer corridor and the shrine of the
Goddess are submerged in sand. There is a long inscription
in Sanskrit which tells us that King Vishnuvardhana having
routed Adiyaman, the Chola Viceroy, from Talakad, set up
the God, Kirtinarayana, in 1117 AD.

The only temple left unsubmerged is that of
Vaidyeswara, built of granite in the Dravidian style. Facing
east, it has a beautifully sculptured outer wall. The temple
has figures of the gods in Shiva's family. On the central
ceiling in the hall are represented various aspects and acts of
Shiva. There are two stone images in front of the temple of
the brothers Tala and Kadu, two brothers from whom this
place derives its name. The brothers one day saw in the
forest a tree being worshipped by wild elephants. Stirred by
curiosity they began to cut down the tree. From the wound
inflicted by the axe flowed blood, and peering through the
cut they saw a lingam within the tree. A voice commanded
them to dress the wound with the leaves of the tree,
whereupon there was a flow of milk instead of blood. They
drank the milk and were transformed into celestial beings;
the elephants (which were sages in transformation) also
drank the milk and were transported to Kailasa; and the
place became known as Talakad. The temple is dedicated to
Vaidyeswara, that is Iswara who has the medicament.

The sandy deluge was caused by a woman's curse when
the place was conquered by a Mysore Raja in 1634.

Tirumal Raya, the representative of the Vijayanagar court at Seringapatam, fell ill seriously, and came to Talakad in order to seek relief by performing certain rites at the shrine of Vaidyeswara. His wife, Rangamma, was in charge of the government at Seringapatam in his absence. One day she heard that her husband's condition had grown worse and hastened to his side, handing over Seringapatam and its dependencies to Raja Wodeyar, the Mysore ruler. So far there seems to be dependable history; beyond this there is much vague and fantastic legend. It is said that there was in the possession of the Rani a rare bit of jewellery, which was much coveted by Raja Wodeyar. He gathered an army and marched on Talakad in order to obtain the jewellery. The sick viceroy fell in action. Saddened and enraged, the Rani went to the river bank, flung the piece of jewellery far into the river, and drowned herself opposite to Malingi (a large town on the other bank of Kaveri, one of the seven of which Talakad was composed after the twelfth century) with the following curse on her lips:

> *'Let Talakad become sand,*
> *Let Malingi become a whirlpool, and*
> *Let the Mysore Rulers beget no heirs.'*

A woman's curse is potent, and the sands crept on the city; and where the old town of Malingi stood, there is seen now only the eddying waters of Kaveri.

SOMANATHPUR

Somanatha, an officer under the Hoysala king Narasimha III (1254-1291 AD) established this village giving it his name. It is about 48 km from Mysore, the road passing through Thirumakudlu-Narasipur, a little town at the charming spot where the rivers Kaveri and Kapini meet. Somanathpur is a very insignificant village today, but it presents to us a work of art which offers us a moment's escape into an ancient day, as do the temples at Belur and Halebid. Of this temple Lewis Rice says: 'This elaborately carved structure is attributed to Jakanachari, the famous sculptor and architect of the Hoysala kings, under whom Hindu art in Mysore reached its culmination. Though not on the scale of the unfinished temple at Halebid, the general effect is more pleasing, from the completion of the superstructure, consisting of three pyramidal towers or *Vimana* surmounting the triple shrine; . . . Round the exterior base are portrayed consecutively, with considerable spirit, the leading incidents in the *Ramayana, Mahabharatha*, and *Bhagavata*, carved in potstone, the termination of each chapter and section being indicated respectively by a closed or half-closed door. The number of separate sculptured images erected upon and around the basement, whose mutilated remains are shown around, was no less than 74.'

SIVASAMUDRAM

Here the Kaveri divides into two branches, forming the island of Sivasamudram, and descends into the plains of

Tamil Nadu in two falls, Gagana Chukki and Bara Chukki. Gagana Chukki is on the western branch of the river, forming the boundary between Mysore and Coimbatore. It is about three kilometers from the Travellers' Bungalow. Here the river hurls down the precipice about two hundred feet, roaring, foaming, and spraying, into a deep pool below. The eastern branch, Bara Chukki, during the rainy season, falls over the hill-side in a continuous sheet, nearly a mile broad; and this, set in a forest land, provides a sight which for sheer beauty and magnificence is excelled only by Jog Falls.

This island town was founded in the sixteenth century by one Ganga Raja. There was a serious omission in the inauguration rites, and the line was doomed to extinction after the third generation. Ganga Raja's reign was prosperous and long lasting. After him came his son Nandi Raja, whose mind was obsessed with the doom that hung over the family. One day he called up his wife to go with him and see Gagana Chukki, which was in floods. As they rode up the steep rock, the queen's heart beat fast and she asked why he was riding so recklessly. He didn't hear her. His mind was fixed on the atonement he was going to make for the omission at the inauguration. He urged the horse on. The cliff over which the river leapt swung on view; the roaring of Gagana Chukki drowned all the terrified questioning and pleading of his wife crouched beside him on the horse; they approached the edge, gallopped over, and plunged headlong with the cataract. Ganga Raja II who succeeded him had a prosperous and quiet reign. He had two daughters whom he gave in marriage to two chieftains in the neighbourhood. This alliance deprived the chieftains of all tranquillity and happiness, for their wives constantly nagged them, contrasting their husbands' conditions with the splendour and the power of their father. Incensed by this they combined and evolved a plan to humble their wives and prove their own superiority. They assembled their forces and besieged Sivasamudram. The siege lasted twelve years; and yet they were not able to enter the island. In the end they corrupted the minister of Ganga Raja, and he sent away the guards at the ford on some prolonged errand. The enemy poured into the place while Ganga Raja's attention was concentrated on a game of chess with his minister. The excited shouting and noise made by the soldiers reached the king's ears at last and he rose to his feet. The minister explained that it was the noise of children at play, and requested him to sit down and continue the game. But the king kicked away the chess pieces, drew his sword and killed all the women and children in the palace; he then rushed forward to meet the invaders and was killed fighting. The sons-in-law who had not expected such a holocaust but only wanted to prove their worth to their wives, were horrified at the turn of events. They jumped on their horses and gallopped at full speed towards Gagana Chukki and went over; which example was immediately followed by their wives, whose inordinate pride in their parent had been responsible for the working out of the curse on the family. In the end the extinction was complete.

The dashing cataract presented itself as a facility for picturesque suicides to old kings, but to a modern mind it appealed as a thing that could be usefully employed. One Edmund Carrington, an electrical engineer, applied in 1894 for permission to utilize the energy of the falls. And today Sivasamudram is one of the most famous electricity generating stations in India. Other hydro-electric schemes in Karnataka and outside may be more advanced in many ways, but Sivasamudram Power Station has to its credit the fact that it is one of the earliest power houses in the country and has a place in the history of hydro-electric development in India.

'It is just about a century since Michael Faraday made his fundamental discoveries in electromagnetism on which the whole modern practice of electrical generation is based, but it was not until Thomas Edison invented the incandescent lamp about 1890 that electric lighting became universally possible. About the time Edison invented the incandescent lamp, a commercial type of motor was developed. These inventions and developments immediately made extremely flexible the production, distribution and use of electrical energy for all classes of lighting and for motive power purposes.

'It did not take the Mysore Government very long after these investigations and developments to appreciate the value of hydro-electric power and to start an investigation of her resources. The survey of the hydro-power resources of the Mysore State actually began in 1898, about ten years after the invention of the incandescent lamp and the development of an economical motor.'—Mr S. G. Forbes (Chief Electrical Engineer).

MELKOTE

A sacred place about 48 km from Mysore, built on the rocky hills, Yadugiri, overlooking the Kaveri valley. Here the great teacher, Ramanujacharya, took shelter from his persecutors and stayed for about fourteen years. Ramanuja was born at Sri Perambatur, studied at Conjeevaram, and retired to Srirangam, which is at the parting of the rivers Kaveri and Coleroon. In that seclusion he evolved his system of philosophy and wrote his great works.

He then travelled far and wide spreading his doctrine and establishing several *maths*, with the chief one at Ahobila. His preachings and conversion brought him in conflict with the Chola king who was a staunch Saiva. The king proclaimed that all the Brahmins in the dominion should declare their faith in Siva, and those who could not do this were persecuted. At this, Ramanuja fled from the Tamil province, and was given asylum by Bittiga, the Hoysala king, who came under the influence of this teacher and was converted to Vaishnavism and assumed the name 'Vishnuvardhana'.

The principal temple at Melkote is the one dedicated to Sri Krishna, under the name of *Chella Pillai*, meaning 'darling son'. Buchanan, in his journal, has an explanation for it. When Ramanuja went to the shrine to perform puja, he found the idol missing and was told that it had been carried away by the 'turc' king of Delhi. Ramanuja went to Delhi and found that the king had given it to his daughter for her to play with. The girl had fallen deeply in love with this handsome image and would not easily part with it. But the power of a *mantra* uttered by Ramanuja brought the image into his hands. He clasped it close to his body, calling it 'Chella Pillai', and returned to Melkote. The broken-hearted princess mounted a horse and followed him as fast as she could. When she was about to reach out her hand for the idol she disappeared and was never seen again. A monument was built for the princess at the foot of the hill.

On the summit of the hill is the Narasimha temple, richly endowed, and possessing a very valuable collection of jewels. In 1614 Raja Wodeyar made over to the temple a large estate he received from the Vijayanagar king, Venkatapathi Raya. Even Tippu Sultan granted some elephants for the temple. The chief annual celebration is the *Vairamudi* festival, which is attended by tens and thousands of people. This is a celebration of the recovery of the diamond crown of Vishnu which was stolen by a serpent and carried off to a distant world underground; Vishnu's great devotee and vehicle, Garuda, the divine eagle, destroyed the demon snake and retrieved the diamond crown.

GOLD MINE

Sitting on a stool near a bunk we are waiting for a lift to come up. Rescue Party Instructions and Safety First Principles meet the eye everywhere. There is an 'Accident Board' on which are written the names of miners who have gone down and had accidents. 'The accident per thousand is about—, very much less than the road accidents in London', says the Inspector of Mines, reading my mind as I look at the board. Everything here has an air of danger and accident. Safety First is the religion here.

Suddenly a door opens where there was nothing a moment ago and a couple of men wearing metal hats come out, blinking in the daylight. They at once acquire a strange interest, beings who have been underground for hours picking gold! The lift is ready for us. I go into the bunk and sign an agreement absolving the company from all responsibility for my life and limbs. It is not very easy to sign a document of this kind. 'I am burying myself; if I don't come out again I have only myself to thank for it.' Is this my last moment in life?

'Do you go down fairly often?' I ask.

'Certainly, every day; it is my business,' says the gentleman; and this is reassuring: his casualness is encouraging. He goes down every day; so people do come up. I sign the agreement. After that I am given a skull cap and a sort of hat made of bamboo splinters. I try to evade it, because I know I look ridiculous with it on. But my friend won't hear of it. 'We never permit anyone to go down unless they put these on. It is a protection for the head from falling stones.' He picks up a lamp and we step into a lift; the door is chained up by an attendant. The lift starts down. Through the perforations in the lift I see patches of light dashing past and disappearing. We find ourselves in utter darkness, eerily lit up by the lamp.

'We are going down at the rate of 100 feet per minute,' says the officer. I see nothing going past except the wooden supports of the shaft walls. Here I am racing down. Who will know I am here? Suppose something happens to the cable and we get stuck here, going neither down nor up. Slow suffocation in there like an ant put in a matchbox and buried. And so on grow my morbid imaginings. (I learn later that there is an alternative steam-controlled arrangement always in readiness to step in if electricity should fail for any length of time.)

There is a slight heaviness in the chest and my ears grow dull. I can't follow what my friend is saying. 'Are you feeling funny about the ear? It is due to the great pressure we are in. . . . We are now at sea level . . . We are below sea level now, a thousand feet below sea level.' The lift comes to a stop, the door opens, and we step into a strange world. Controls, trolley lines, trollies, workmen, and officers—it is an extremely busy place. My friend takes me to the mouth of another shaft. 'This shaft leads further down 4,000 feet, i.e. 8,000 and odd feet from the surface.' My head reels. The height of Nilgiris upside down. This makes it the deepest mine in the world. Compared to it the level where we stand appears to be the sunlit world on top, though it is 4,000 odd feet deep; the temperature is around 90° or 100°F. Since I am not sure of being able to bear the temperature and pressure further down, I decline his offer to take me further down.

Through curving tunnels we pass, pushing heavy steel doors, which opened, let into the tunnel a powerful gust of wind. Jagged rocks overhead and around, walls from which the ore has been removed, and supported by heavy timber and iron. A cloud of dust envelops us, the light grows dull in it.

'Dust is coming up this way, Sir,' says someone appearing before us suddenly like an apparition. 'Let us turn back and go because it will take time for it to clear.' More iron doors opening and shutting and we are in another section. The same jagged rocks, trolley lines, and a vague darkness ahead. It is disappointing to one who has thought of a gold mine as a place where glittering nuggets lie scattered about.

'Which is the gold ore?' A whitish line running along the rock is being pointed out to me. It is not more impressive than metal heaped on roadside. I feel an admiration for the first human being who could connect this stone with gold. After the blasting, these portions have been left over because these are not worth the cost of removal. The sides are supported by heavy beams, piled up; some portions of the beam look crushed and flattened, like a matchbox trodden upon, due to the pressure that the earth goes on exerting from above. In some places where the logs cannot stand the pressure circular iron bands are added to reinforce and hold the roof up.

As the lift seizes us and takes us upward I cannot help feeling proud of being a human being. The whole organization is a triumph of man's ingenuity and courage in the face of something which outsizes him and can often outwit him by defeating his calculations. The jagged walls of the tunnel which might close in any moment, the lift which might stick, the gas which might blow up, and a dozen other things—and against these man's confidence in his machines and mathematics, and his stubbornness in getting out of the earth what he wants on his own terms.

Vague hints of daylight through the holes in the lift. We are approaching the top. When the lift comes to a stop I am quite happy to be back on good old surface.

The above is a description of an experience undergone many years ago, but I have verified and found that the actual operations of going up and down and of cutting the ore have not changed substantially—only more men are at work now and the mines are deeper. I am including an extract from a report by the Managing Director, Bharat Gold Mines Limited, which gives us the latest picture:

'Bharat Gold Mines Limited, with about 100 years of experience, has developed excellent mining culture and high traditions which make us pioneers in hard-rock deep mining. We have at KGF about 800 miles of tunnels underground driven for over 100 years. Also from the inception of these mines upto January 1977, approximately 45.05 million tonnes of gold-bearing ore has been extracted from these mines yielding about 779.4 tonnes of gold. Present targeted production stands at about 4,00,000 tonnes of ore and 22,00,000 grammes of gold per annum.'

KOLAR

Kolar is rich in history. It was founded by the Gangas early in the Christian Era. In 1004 Kolar passed into the hands of Cholas, and in the next century came under the Hoysalas. In the fifteenth century Timme Gowda, given the title of Chikka Rayal, was authorized by the Vijayanagar king to repair the fort of Kolar. The Bijapur king next held the place, and in 1639 Shahaji, father of Shivaji, became the governor of this district, and half a century later the Mughals took it. Fatte Muhamud, father of Haidar Ali became Faujdar of Kolar under the Subedar of Sira. Kolar was ceded to Haidar Ali in 1761, changed hands once again and was finally restored to Tippu in 1792.

Buchanan who travelled in these parts in the early part of the nineteenth century gives us a fairly good idea of the place in those days. Kolar was surrounded by a large mud fort, the town had 700 houses, many of which were inhabited by weavers. On the hill were four small villages having their own fields, gardens and tanks. At Antara Ganga there was an annual assemblage of about 10,000 persons. The villages round about were generally surrounded by small fortifications for protection against

Bedars who, professing to be servants of the Palegar in the neighbourhood, invaded the villages at night and committed robbery. Whenever such persons were seen, signal was given by the sentry in the watch tower and the robbers were fired on.

Today, Kolar is a prosperous town, with signs of development and growth on every side.

About three kilometers from the town is situated a fine sweep of hills called Kolar Betta or Satasringa Parvatha; the highest point rises to a height of 1230 meters above the sea level. On the east side of the hill is a perennial spring named Antara Ganga; the water issues from the mouth of stones resembling Basava and is held to be sacred. This is believed to be the scene of Renuka's *sati* and Parasurama's vow.

MULBAGAL

Thirty kilometers from Kolar. It is known as the eastern gate because it is on the road to Tirupati. Pilgrims to Tirupati go through a preliminary ceremony of shaving, and bathing in Narasimha Tirtha before proceeding further. There is an interesting tomb of a Mohammadan saint called Haider Wali, which attracts a large number of pilgrims during the annual celebrations. Four miles from Mulbagal is Kudu-male, at the foot of which are the ruins of large temples, the most prominent of them being those of Someswara and Ganesha. The sculptures in these are attributed to Jakanachari. The gods, it is said, going to make war on Tripura assembled their forces on this hill, and hence its name: the Hill of Assembly. Another village in this taluk which is of great antiquity is Avani, about 12 km from Mulbagal. It is identified to be Avantika, one of the ten sacred places in India. It is believed that Valmiki, the author of Ramayana, lived here; Rama on his way back from Lanka remained here for some time; Sita after she had been banished came here and gave birth to her twin sons, Lava and Kusa, who were protected by Valmiki and brought up. There are many temples here dedicated to various personages in Ramayana.

NANDI HILLS

A popular summer resort in the west of the district. The summit is over 1300 meters in height. Sir Mark Cubbon was responsible for making this place habitable and popular. The first few houses were built in his time. There is a temple of Sacred Bull on top, known as Yoga Nandiswara and another known as Boga Nandiswara at the village of Nandi down below. Both these temples are of great architectural beauty and have been in existence since the time of Cholas, Pallavas, and Hoysalas. Around the summit are ruins of fortifications erected by Haidar and Tippu.

KELADI CHIEFS

On the outskirts of Sagar in Shimoga District, are Keladi and Ikkeri, at present two obscure villages, which were the capital of Bednur chiefs, who ruled these parts in the fifteenth century, and maintained their power for nearly three centuries. The most famous name in the dynasty was Sivappa Nayak whose conquests extended as far as

Shimoga in the east and Kanara in the west, and whose expeditions extended from Balam to Vastra, Sakkrepatna, and Hassan. His most memorable act was granting protection to Sri Ranga Raya, the fugitive king of Vijayanagar, in 1646, and he even tried to attack Seringapatam on his behalf.

Keladi has charming anecdotes about the founding of the Nayak's Empire. Two brothers Chavuda Gowda (1499-1513) and Badra Gowda had two servants, who while cultivating the fields noticed that a cow often went and shed her milk on an ant-hill. On digging the hill, Chavuda Gowda found a lingam and built over it a temple. A few days later, the servants dug up an old sword, and kept it under an old thatch roof, intending to make a scythe of it. Now they discovered that if a bird perched on the roof the sword leapt up in the form of a snake and killed it. This interested Chavuda Gowda who took out the sword, cleaned it, and kept it in his house. A few days later a ploughshare struck some metallic object which was found to be the ring of a cauldron. Chavuda Gowda had a dream in which he was directed to take the treasure in the cauldron after performing human sacrifice to it. When they heard of the dream, the servants begged their master to sacrifice them. Two mounds at the entrance to the village mark the spot where the servants were sacrificed.

Immense wealth, a powerful sword, and the blessings of the deity in the temple, all come his way without his seeking, the Gowda felt that fates were driving him towards more important goals than raising corn. He gathered a small force and subdued the neighbouring villages. News of his exploits reaching Vijayanagar kings, he was taken prisoner and sent to the capital, where he helped his captors quell some local rebellions, which pleased the king and he was released and given back the territories he had already won around Keladi.

Chavuda Gowda later transferred his capital to Ikkeri (1560-1640), which became a flourishing capital. He built a palace of mud and timber, artistically gilded. Not much of this can be seen in Ikkeri now. All that remains of the old grandeur is the Aghoreswara temple, which is a spacious, granite structure. It is empty and silent now, with grass growing on its walls and corridors; a solitary priest appears from somewhere with the keys of the temple, when any visitor calls him up. If we could unwind the reels of time, we might perhaps notice, four hundred years ago, the prestige of the priest of the king's temple, as he arrived for puja while the crowds assembled in the spacious pillared hall waited for him with flowers and incense.

In about 1640, Nagar (then Bednur) became the capital of the chiefs. The town rapidly grew. Its walls were thirteen kilometers in circumstance and had ten gates, with the palace of the king on a hill at the centre of the town. A foreign traveller visiting it nearly a century after it was founded wrote: 'The Bednur Prince is much more magnificent and powerful than those of Malabar. His kingdom produces many peculiar commodities, such as sandal-wood, which is found there in great abundance, as well as rice. . . . The city (Bednur) where the Raja holds his court lies some leagues inland, and is connected with the sea port by a fine road, planted with trees, which the inhabitants are obliged to keep in excellent order. This road is so secure that any stranger might go and sleep there with bags full of money, and nobody would molest or rob him, for if such a thing occurred the people in the neighbourhood would not only be severely punished, but would be forced to make good the money.' In 1763 Bednur was captured by Haidar Ali. 'The Keladi, Ikkeri, or Bednur State, was the most considerable of those absorbed into the present Mysore territories by the victories of Haidar Ali, and its conquest was always acknowledged by him to have established his fortune.'—Lewis Rice.

BELGAUM, DHARWAR AND HUBLI

As a little change from my own descriptions, I asked artist Laxman to record his impressions for me of these places.

In a note Laxman says: 'These three towns, somehow, form a sort of Trinity in one's mind and in retrospect one merges in the other. Their histories seem to follow the same pattern as others, starting with a legendary association and then on to a rule of the early Hindu Kingdoms, Rashtrakutas, Kadambas etc. and then routine invasions by Bijapur Sultanates, Mugals, Maharattas, Haidar, Tippu and the British. Still these three towns have a charm of their own, owing to their elevation, and the landscape is very pleasant.

'Belgaum interested me very much, among other reasons, for its proximity and association with Kittur where Rani Chennamma created history by resisting the British as far back as 1824 fighting from her citadel; she rejected the British Collector, Thackeray's order on the question of an adoption since she was childless and wished to nominate a successor for the Principality. In that engagement,

Thackeray was killed, along with his soldiers. Thereafter Chennamma was taken prisoner and died in 1829.

*

'I found in Dharwar a number of churches all of early nineteenth century, and I was also interested to learn about Karnataka Varthaga Sanga started in 1890; a number of very impressive mosques, and temples. The most important institution in Dharwar is the Karnataka University occupying an area of 283 acres. Its achievements and activities are frequently mentioned in conversation, people here are justifiably proud of their University.

'Hubli, thirteen miles from Dharwar, is mentioned in old records as a place of large wealth and great trade, inviting plunderers. In ancient times, a large trade was carried on in sandalwood and ivory, and from Goa, silk, cotton, wool and rice were imported. The tradition of Industry and Commerce continues even today. Cotton mills, Ginning and Pressing Factories, Railway Workshop and schools and colleges are important landmarks in Hubli.

'Now on to Bijapur. Whenever people talked about Gol Gumbuz and its whispering gallery, I had paid no attention believing the account was the usual reluctance of the tourist to face disappointment with the place he visited after spending so much money and energy. But I was astonished beyond belief when a voice spoke to me almost from inside my ear! It was the guide whispering to me from across the circular gallery some 140 feet or so away! I heard crumpling of a piece of paper, striking of a match and his watch ticking away. People thronged here to whisper to each other, laugh at the thrill of it all, sing and shout for the mere joy of hearing their voice echo and re-echo seven times. The poor Sultan and his family who built it lay in their tombs shrouded in white below in the enormous hall and were of secondary importance.

'Bijapur, of course, could not go without its quota of fortresses and gun placements. I saw a Big Bertha of a cannon atop a fort. It was massive and ugly. I thought that, more than its firing capability, Tippu must have had trust in its appearance to destroy the enemy more effectively.

*

'Dandeli was a green lush wilderness teeming with tigers, bisons and other wildlife, I was told. I had arrived at night and even in the darkness I could sense the denseness of the jungle. But the first thing the daylight revealed was a chimney belonging to the West Coast Paper Mill with billowing smoke. Then I saw a mountainous raw stock of bamboo. I was told that bamboo was becoming scarce. No wonder, I thought. What about the tigers, wild beasts and birds? Oh, they have gone away to the other end of the forest, as there are too many trucks and jeeps moving about. At the other end dynamiting was going on to build a dam to impound Kalinadi for the Project. The Chief Engineer took me through the tunnel in the belly of the mountain, and it was a unique and eerie experience. The drive from Dandeli to Karwar was one of the finest. On the way I halted at Supa, a tiny hamlet and had tea sitting in the veranda of a typical colonial type Travellers' Bungalow overlooking the river Kali. I was told there was a temple of Surpanakha,* (only one of its kind in the world—hence Supa) submerged somewhere under the water. The local

---

* A demoness, sister of Ravana.

belief was that it emerged once in a few decades to satisfy Surpanakha's devotees. Of course, it might be one of those stories one heard all the time in these parts. While leaving the cottage I discovered a small marble tablet stating the year it was built—1873. I was greatly saddened to leave it, for in my next visit, it would not be there. This piece of colonial charm and the village Supa will be under 300 feet of water when the dam is built.

'Karwar was a typically sea-side scenic town; merry fisher-folk, sailboats, blue sea, nylon nets and the smell of drying fish, sandy beaches, palm groves, islands and lighthouse and coves. It could become an excellent tourist spot like the nearby Goa. The run from here to Mangalore along the seacoast was indescribably picturesque.'

KALINADI POWER PROJECT

About Kalinadi Pourer Project, I cannot do better than quote from a booklet entitled *March of Karnataka*, written by a senior officer of Government of Karnataka.

The State has enormous untapped potentiai. It has a power potential of 5500 MW of which hardly 18 per cent has been developed so far. Realizing the importance of optimum development of power, both for industrialisation and for the green revolution, the State has set up a Power Development Corporation. This is again a pioneering effort and an organizational innovation for generation of power. The power corporation has been taking comprehensive measures for planning and production of power with a view to overcoming any shortage of power in the coming years. It is presently implementing the Kalinadi Hydro-Electric Project which has been planned to develop in Stage-1 910 MW and over 4,000 million units of energy annually. The energy will cost about 3 paise per unit, one of the lowest in the country. The commissioning of the Project by 1978 is crucial to the power supply position in the State.

Postscript

have traversed, literally speaking, much ground in the foregoing chapters from Raichur at one end to Somanathpur at the other, from Chamarajanagar to Kolar, covering several hundred kilometers, and I have described the scenes, histories, the cultural heritage, and whatever seemed to me worthwhile in each place. Now what follows is in the nature of an 'Afterword' if such a term is permissible, when one has stepped down from the rostrum and lowered one's voice to utter an informal aside or a piece of criticism, perhaps after sounding solemn and serious all along. 'I expected you to write in a lighter vein,' says a reader, 'but I found you too serious all through!' 'That can't be helped, my friend,' I explain. 'There are certain aspects of life which will not lend themselves to lighter treatment. In dealing with the subject of Karnataka one is overwhelmed with the weight of history. A narration of historical events cannot but sound grim. One cannot joke about bloody conflicts and conquests.'

In writing a book of this kind, one's problem is to find a *via media* between objective and subjective treatment. In a journal of travels one could expatiate upon one's experiences purely from a personal angle,—the joy one felt, the discomfort, blunders one could have avoided, the comedy one witnessed in a strange character or a situation, and a general criticism of circumstances. But that would be part of an autobiography, rather than an account of places and persons one has seen. Although I could not completely

135

avoid personal impressions in certain parts of this book, I
have, on the whole, tried to be impersonal. In this chapter,
however, I intend to record my views unreservedly on one
or two pet subjects.

A new brand of 'trouble-maker' (according to
administrators and industrialists) has become prominent
since a decade, who constantly protests and questions, 'At
what price?', wherever he sees natural resources being
exploited. He is the 'Environmentalist' or 'Conservationist'.
Call him what you will, but he is the one who takes a long
view, not concerning himself with immediate benefits or
priorities. The forests of Karnataka provide all the riches
that a wood-lover might dream of: the finest teak,
rosewood, sandalwood, and bamboo, not to mention other
kinds. There was a time I remember, while travelling in a
bus towards Ooty or over Dhimbam Ghats, one passed
through dense forests flanking the road: the broad-leaves of
the teak, filigree of bamboo clusters, and a variety of
creepers, climbers and miscellaneous vegetation, forming
an impenetrable screen, with a foot-track winding through
and vanishing mysteriously into the thicket. Today the
scene has changed. Timber prematurely cut and utilized in
the urgency of the World War II actually started the
depletion of wood. After the War, came the industrialist,
looking for wood-pulp for the manufacture of paper and
artificial yarn, or softwood for boxing and crating his
produce. His hunger for raw material was insatiable and
unless the forests were continuously denuded, his factories
would come to a standstill. Fuel contractors and poachers
also contributed their share of devastation of forest land
without a qualm. The industrialist, at least, undertakes to
replant as much as he destroys, which, however, does not

amount to more than a technical satisfaction since the rate of destruction is visible and calculable but not the rate of regrowth: the whole thing appears to be merely a stock register affair—a tree for a tree to set the records straight. Nowadays when I travel over the same mountain roads I mentioned a while ago, I see eucalyptus where bamboo trees swayed before. I cannot help feeling that I am being cheated with a fake account. Eucalyptus, whatever may be its worth medicinally, cannot be a substitute for bamboo in any sense. Bamboo, among its other benefits, helps the preservation of elephants too by providing them shelter and nourishment. Has anyone heard of an elephant standing beside a eucalyptus tree or chewing its leaves? I don't know. When I travel through the Karnataka forests, whether in Coorg, Malnad, Mysore, or Dandeli, I notice everywhere steady emasculation of bamboo, and feel depressed. It is no satisfaction to be told that some pests also attack bamboo and are responsible for their depletion. I fear that a twig laboriously acquired and preserved in a drawing room, may be the only means of displaying a specimen of bamboo to the coming generations. I cannot put pen to paper nowadays without thinking of all the cutting, crushing and destruction, that has gone on in order to provide me a sheet of white paper. One now realizes the significance of Valmiki's sloka at the beginning of the Ramayana where he says, 'Man, the destroyer, who will not let innocent birds mate in peace'.

Our mountains and hills have to be saved too. Of course hacking them for mineral ores or tunneling through them may be a necessary evil, in a modern culture which is based on commerce and trade rather than aesthetics. It was quite nightmarish to listen to the philosophy of an engineer in charge of a project: 'Oh! Mountains are no problems. Give me the men, machinery, and power, and I can guarantee to scoop the inside of any mountain and convert it into a mere shell. I read in a recent American Journal that they have developed a chemical process by which a mountain can be reduced to fine powder and flushed off into the sea. No problem is too great for an engineer today. I am second to none in my love of a mountain, but when necessary I can move it or make my way through it for whatever purpose . . .' This man is not a man, but a giant or a superman, whose prowess should no doubt be utilized for the prosperity of our country but without letting him go too far. Otherwise, he may flake off layers of Deccan Plateau and reduce it to a dust bowl below sea level.

Mountain-tops, valleys, downs and uplands, beaches and plains, compose the picture of Karnataka. No other part of India can offer such scenic variety, clothed in every kind of vegetation from lantana shrub to the towering *baliga* trees growing up to two hundred feet, harbouring abundant wildlife including serpent variety from the fourteen-foot Hamadrayad on Agumbe slopes to the slender green snake peering over a wayside hedge. All creatures have a right to exist on this planet side by side with man, of course at a proper distance from each other. Modern developments and projects are threatening to render animals homeless. I have mentioned this only as a problem without being able to offer a solution. I can now almost hear the remark, 'Should we go back to cave-dwelling and live on berries and roots or turn Cubbon Park over to tigers and bears?' I have no answer to such a remark but have only this to say: 'Surely there must be a way of utilizing resources without wiping out the sources.'

Karnataka has a versatile background, which has been a source of inspiration to its poets, mystics and minstrels; and for the founding of different centres of religion. The stones and rocks have facilitated the development of its architecture and sculpture. Its open spaces and equable climate have nurtured sports and games and brought forth many a sportsman of national and international calibre. Its countryside has fostered, even to this day, unique cultural modes such as Yakshagana, shadow and puppet plays and folk drama.

It must be our ambition to protect and preserve our riches to the maximum extent possible.

Appendices

Appendix 1

THE KHEDDA

(This was a radio feature I wrote years ago, at a time when along with the Dasara and the Birthday celebrations of the Maharaja, the Khedda was the most important event in Mysore attracting visitors from all over the country. The Khedda operations at Karapur [60 miles from Mysore] were conducted in order to trap elephants through a highly specialized and complex technique before thousands of spectators. Now all that area of elephant activity is under water following the completion of Kabini Project, and Mysore has lost one of its grandest occasions.
It is included as a nostalgic piece, and a sort of historical memento.)

In the heaven of children's vision, you have a never-ending ride on the back of an elephant, and are privileged to watch an unceasing march past of elephants. In real life, the tinkling bell of a passing elephant attracts all children to the street. No child ever lets one pass its house without suggesting, 'Why not call it in?' and if the elders are sportive, the elephant comes in, with the mahout perched on it, and accepts a coconut and a pat on his trunk, and trumpets and salams, and goes his tinkling way again. This institution is as old as humanity, at least in this part of the country. However, it is just a pretence to say that elephants fascinate only children. I don't think any normal adult ever outgrows it!

Mysore, more than any other city, presents this spectacle oftener and all the year round. The reason is not far to seek. It is a common belief in this part of the country that all well-bred elephants come from Kakankote Forest, almost fifty miles from the City. Kakankote is really a portion of the vast belt of jungle on the Western Ghats. Gradually as one approaches it, one's road becomes hemmed in with gigantic natural fencing of bamboos, so thick that you see nothing beyond. But part the clumps and pass in, a few yards off, about twenty feet below your level you will find a broad river, which is called Kabini, flowing on smoothly, and the opposite bank slopes up, imperceptibly merging in a small range of hillocks about ten miles away. With this part of Kabini river as the centre if you draw a circle to enclose say about ten miles, there you have the natural home of elephants. They breed and grow in herds, feeding on a rich store of long grass, foliage, and bamboo, and wallowing in the cool waters of Kabini. The system of Khedda may be defined as one of watching, hemming in, and driving the elephant herd across the river into stockades. Stated thus, it conveys none of the excitement and extra-ordinary amount of planning it involves. To understand it fully let us see it through the eyes of a Head of the Forest Department, who undertakes to direct this activity. On a certain day while he is in his office at Bangalore he decides that a herd of elephants must be rounded up. They may be multiplying fast, or they may be ravaging the neighbouring field or villages; or elephants may be required for trade or ceremonial purposes. One or the other of all these reasons may operate and one fine day in a conference in his office the Chief of the Forest Department decides that he will capture a herd during their next breeding season, that is, sometime between October end and January when the monsoon has ceased and new leaves have sprouted in the jungle.

To say, 'We shall round up the elephant herd', sounds simple, but the moment he has said it, he gets involved in a set of complicated activities, which combine both field operations and work at the office desk. Of course a file starts growing. Men are sent out to observe and report on the strength of the herd or of groups seen here and there, and of their movement.

The Kakankote area gradually undergoes a change. People begin to arrive and depart. Several trained elephants, known as *kumkies* (invaluable allies of man in the task of capturing and training elephants) with their mahouts, start coming, and all day the sound of their bells are heard in the jungle. Small bamboo hutments spring up and begin to be peopled; a tent colony develops in the clearing. Construction goes on along the river, platform or tree-forks, for affording special angle for photographers, and seating accommodation on the river bank for hundreds of visitors, who will come on the day of the drive. In addition to it plenty of work on the construction of the stockade with hefty poles lashed together with twisted coir ropes. The stockade starts at a point on the river bank, with a drop-gate, and develops into an enclosure of half a mile circumference: at one end it is narrowed down, with platforms built above, from where the public may view the roping of elephants after they are caught. Soon a date is fixed for the actual drive of the herd into the stockade. As the date of the drive approaches, the orbit of the movement of the elephants is narrowed down by a corps of about two thousand men of all categories. How this is accomplished is a highly technical matter. We are bound to hear a great deal of 'Drive Lines' and 'Surround' and such other terms, when we ask the question, 'How do you manage to encircle the herd and keep it where you want it?' It is a highly technical process. A 'surround' is the perimeter area within which a herd is observed and kept, and the drive lines are those that get closer within which the herd is moved from stage to stage; it is achieved by various means, by lighting fire, by firing guns or sounding clappers, and by generally determining not to let the herd get past a certain boundary.

A regular chart develops regarding the position of the elephant herd. By a look at the paper on the table one may say how many are there in the herd, approximately, and where they are at any given moment. The camp begins to look more and more like a General's desk during a campaign; papers are scrutinized and signed, a variety of persons come in with reports and receive instructions and go out of sight. Nearby the kumkie's bells agitate the silence. The tension increases. That the drive should go through as planned becomes the chief obsessing thought in everyone. Many problems present themselves with a lot of acuteness now. Rumour comes of a single elephant roaming in the vicinity trying to draw away the herd. A single elephant may mean anything. It creates a delicate situation, to say nothing worse. The wanderer may be a member of the herd who may be out on a little expedition of his own, and who must not be denied the chance to return to his fold with the return of good sense; he cannot be handled roughly. In the latest Khedda a most taxing problem was created by the presence of a lone elephant in the outskirts, and the foresters tried to entice him into captivity with the help of a female elephant, named Radha Pyari, but he did not succumb to the charms of this lady, and caused many moments of anxiety till he was driven outside the pale. Apart from this the health and temperament of the thousands of workers and their morale is all-important. And above all, the rain god should not turn his attention to this part of the earth. The Khedda is no doubt arranged only when monsoon has ceased, but one can never be sure. Rain has a habit of descending when it is least wanted.

Everything is set and ready, and as a measure of vast crowds that are expected, already a coffee restaurant has sprung up at the entrance to the jungle. Everywhere you see bamboo: bamboo for walls and roofs of hutments, bamboo for camouflage purposes, bamboo for pontoon bridge, and bamboo for clappers whose rattle keeps the elephants moving. Here and there we see groups of beaters and watchers, two thousand of them are engaged on the job at this moment, sitting around cooking their food or resting. These men have lived with elephants in their natural surroundings all their lives, and play an important role in the Khedda operations. Lorries come and go, cars arrive, and depart. Sign boards spring up here and there, indicating car-park, halts, and enclosures, and so forth. We call on the chief of this campaign. He is in battle dress, shirt sleeves and khaki, and looks careworn and anxious. We ask the same set of questions again and again.

He patiently answers all our questions.

'Where is the herd now?'

'About a couple of miles on that side of the river. The herd was moved just this morning across the river. . .'

'How many do you hope to catch?'

'May be about sixty . . . We can't be definite.'

'Will you be able to get all of them in?'

'I believe so. . . or . . . ,' he trails away in doubt.

'What time does the drive begin . . . ?'

'Half past two . . . if all goes well.'

'How long will it go on?'

'I wish I could tell you that . . . it is all so uncertain, if the herd follows our schedule, we can close the gates at 3.30, but . . .'

'Well, do things ever go wrong?'

'Oh, quite often . . . In my own experience we have had to abandon the project after starting a drive. . . . We are proceeding only on certain assumptions about the behaviour of elephants but if they decide to change their minds and go away nothing can stop them, they will just break through the lines and escape into the jungle; they may refuse to move in the directions we want them to move, they may climb the bank where we don't want them . . . anything may happen, I wouldn't be definite till about this time tomorrow . . .'

'Please tell us when we shall see them march up the river . . .'

He spreads out a plan of the jungle and the river and explains perhaps for the fiftieth time that day, 'This is the river, at this point elephants will be driven . . . they must move up here . . . this is the stockade gate . . . If all goes well it should all be over at three-thirty . . . Mind you, if all goes according to plan . . .'

We leave him. We feel we ought not to bother him anymore.

Following day. Under the banyan tree at the entrance to the jungle, there is a small shrine of Ganesha, the Elephant-faced god, installed about fifty years ago, and no Khedda begins actually without prayer to this god. It is 5 a.m. Prayer at this shrine for the success of the expedition. The Chief Conservator of Forests and his officers and men on elephants, have assembled in front of this shrine for benediction.

(Temple bell mixes on to the sound of several bells and moving away.)

Those are kumkies or trained elephants bearing away the officers and foresters across the Kabini through the morning mist. They are going over to the other bank, where a mile away the elephant herd is kept under observation. They have a great deal to do on the other side before the start of the drive seven hours hence. All the general traffic on the main road ceases at 1 p.m., an hour and a half before the start of the drive. The seats get filled. About 300 chairs are arranged to face the river and camouflaged with foliage. A monkey family, comfortably perched on a high-up bamboo branch, watches the goings-on below with profound interest. They watch the crowd arrive and fill the chairs. They watch parts of the crowd adjourn to the nearby forests with flasks and packed luncheon; they watch microphones getting fixed to the tree branches on the edge of the river.

The hubbub of the expectant crowd increases. Whenever a forest officer is seen he is asked: 'Where exactly do the elephants cross the river?' And he points to a spot on the river on this side of the pontoon. Friends greet each other. Photographers feel their way about and look for vantage points. There is quite a stir. The monkey family above stirs uneasily as forest guards post themselves along the river bank with guns . . . Now an officer of the Forest Department comes up telling the crowd to maintain silence. Silence falls upon the gathering, the tension of expectancy increases. The monkey family shifts uneasily. A crying child is carried off by its disconcerted mother out of earshot. Cameras are trained and ready. At two-thirty the signal for the start of the drive is given as per custom, by the Chief Minister to the Chief Conservator of Forests, who is on the other side of the river, a mile away, waiting to lead the drive personally.

(Sound) (*Telephone conversation*).

Narrator: This is the beginning. (*Gun shots*)

The drive has begun. The crack of a gun, and bugle sound. The monkeys have disappeared. They foresee a hectic time ahead. Bugle and other noises approach. 'Ah, the elephants are over there!' people whisper. A herd makes its appearance on the other side of the river.

They splash water and break twigs on their way. The driving party is behind them urging them on. They are being manoeuvred by the driving party into the exact spot of the river where they are to cross, and then along the river. They come along as if in a spell, a whole herd. A few come up where they are not wanted. Near our part of the river, and the cracks of gun drive them away; the crowd is fascinated by the spectacle of a huge herd going down within a stone's throw. As the wild herd passes, its rear and flank on the other side of the river are closed in by beaters, shouters, noise-makers of all kinds, and trained elephants.

The only direction which is free is being taken by the herd, somewhat bewildered by all this hullabaloo. Their steps lead them on to the point of the river, where the gate of the Khedda is open for them. The leader has no option but to enter it, and the herd follows. The tail of the last elephant disappears into the gate. The drop-gate closes with a bang. The river drive is over. The time is 3.25. The scheduled time was 3.30 p.m. 'If all went well'. Evidently everything has gone on exceedingly well, as if a push-button arrangement had produced out of nowhere, nearly seventy elephants before our eyes. The next stage is the roping of the captives.

And so they are here. It is no doubt, somewhat painful now to watch them being broken in; but it is the pain of education. Kumkies are teachers not traitors. They try to wear out the wildness of wild elephants and make them acceptable in human society. The process of civilization is ever a painful business, at least at the start. And now leaving this stockade, these sixty odd elephants go out into the world—to delight children in zoos and circuses, to lead processions in temples or the palace, and above all help human beings in the performance of hard tasks such as lifting timber in forests. The elephant is man's noble companion—ever gentle and devoted. Khedda has only been a stage in bringing him from his own surroundings into the realms of men.

Appendix 2

WATCHMAN OF THE LAKE

(This one-act play is based on a folk theme, the story of a rustic who sacrificed himself in order to save a tank about to breach. I heard this story sometime ago when I travelled by bus from Kadur to Chikamagalur, while the bus halted indefinitely at a wayside stall selling tender coconuts. At this point I noticed a finger-post pointing 'Sakkrepatna', and made a casual enquiry, which was answered by a fellow passenger with a local anecdote, which I later developed into a one-act play. I have included it in this volume on Karnataka as the folk tradition and the perennial philosophy implicit in the theme are worth our study.)

INTRODUCTION:

On the eastern base of Baba Buden Hills in Karnataka State, there is an obscure little place now called Sakkrepatna, which at one time, a thousand or more years ago, was the capital of a king called Rukmangada. In the centre of this town there is a shrine which is dedicated not to distant gods or heroes but to a rustic, who was watchman of a lake called Ayyankere, four miles from the town. For purposes of this little drama let us call him Mara which is as good as any other name handed down to us by tradition.

152

SCENE ONE

A village at the foot of a hill. Roadmenders at work.

Village Headman:	Go on, boys, go on with your work. Hey, you Racha, why do you stand looking at the sky? You there, you wretched dog, I will push you into the stream if I catch you again gossiping with your neighbour. You dwarf, there, have you no better business than giggling? The road must be ready before the king arrives. Just think: he will be here this time tomorrow. Go on, go on. Anyway what makes you all so merry? Come here, . . . (*commanding*) come here . . . why are you laughing? Tell me, What is it?
Timid Workman :	It is Mara.
Headman :	Ah! Mara, what about him? Is that lunatic anywhere here?
Timid Workman :	Yes, yes, he was behind that rock and peeped at us. When you called he ran away.
Headman :	Where is he? Which way did he go?
Timid Workman :	He sprang off like a buck and ran up the hill.
Headman :	Stop all work. Put down your spades and close round: catch that thief and bring him here. Stun him. if he resists . . . Go . . .

(The workmen throw down their implements and scatter about.)

(They return, crying: 'Master, here he is.')

Headman :	Mara, you worthless dog! Have I not told you to keep away?
Mara :	Yes, my master.
Headman :	What do you mean by disturbing my workmen?
Mara :	I am not disturbing them. I am here on my own business. Let them go on with theirs.
Headman :	Don't talk of your business. Fool! You are a lunatic. Know it. Now go away.
Mara :	Why so?
Headman :	Don't ask. The king will be passing this way and I don't want him to know that our village has fools such as you.
Mara :	I don't feel I am a fool.
Headman :	Now listen. Keep out of our view the next two days, when the king passes this way and back. Otherwise I will have you locked up in the cellar.
Mara :	I will sit there and pray. If that God in the temple thinks I have important work, He will let me out.
Headman :	Now, get out of my presence. You fellows, why do you all stand gaping at me? Get on with your work. . .
Mara :	Once again the Goddess of the river came to me in the dream and said: 'The

king is coming this way. Tell him about the tank. He will listen.'

Headman :	Don't tell me that again, you and your dream. I feel tempted to kick you.
Mara :	What have I said to offend you so much, sir? Are you jealous that the Goddess comes to me rather than to you in dream? Shall I repeat her very words?
Headman :	No. Be off. And like a good fellow keep to your backyard till the king departs. I will give you a fine gift if you behave yourself.
Mara :	Another person has already given me the greatest gift any man could give.
Headman :	Oh! who is that great man?
Mara :	My father-in-law.

(*The workmen laugh at the joke.*)

Headman :	(*Shouting in anger*) Stop laughing everyone! I will starve you all without work if I catch you again laughing at this fellow's mad prattle. Shut up . . . Come here, Bhima. Throw down your crowbar. I have another piece of work for you. Come here.
Bhima :	Yes, master, I have come. What is your command?
Headman :	Bind this fellow hand and foot and throw him in the cellar behind the old

	temple, and keep him there till the day after tomorrow. Do you understand?
Bhima :	Yes, master.
Headman :	Mara, have a look at this giant. He can swing an elephant by its tail. So have a care. If you try any tricks on him, he will crush you out between his thumb and forefinger. . .
Mara :	How did you manage to grow so fat?
Bhima :	My mother gave me iron decoction when I was a baby; and at every dawn I run up the hill with a large grindstone on my back. It is a very big stone. You can't move it even an inch.
Headman :	Here, don't answer his questions. Don't allow him to talk to you.
Mara :	Why not? I too would like to grow fat and strong. If taking iron decoction and carrying grindstones uphill could make me strong, why should I not try it? May be you will not think me mad then.
Bhima :	You can't take the decoction now. Your mother should have put it into you before you were ten days old.
Headman :	Bhima, don't you talk to him. Don't you see he is your prisoner?
Bhima :	Yes, yes. I will be careful hereafter. But who will do my work here?
Headman :	Do not concern yourself with it. You will get your wages all the same, perhaps a quarter more, if you do this bit of work well. Now take him away

156

	and sit over him till the evening of day after tomorrow. Take him away. Drag him like an animal if he gives trouble.
Mara :	No, no, I won't give trouble. I will go with him gladly. Come on, come on. I will tell you all about my dream as we go.
Headman :	Bhima, don't let him do that. He wants to talk to you and slip away 'while you are listening. Now bind up his wrists together with your turban and drag him behind you; gag him if possible . . . Ah, that is good, now it should quieten him. Now begone! . . . How all our time has been wasted! Swing your arms faster . . . You must have the path ready even if you have to work by torches and flares tonight . . .

SCENE TWO

Trumpets blowing, restrained cheering of crowds, etc., announce the arrival of the king. Suddenly there is confusion. As the king is about to pass under a tree, Mara jumps down from its branches. A medley of voices crying, 'Where did he jump from? Who is he? Hold him on . . .'

King :	Silence! Who is this man . . . ?
Answering Voice :	Your gracious Majesty! This man . . .
King :	We will hear the man himself speak.

Answering Voice : Your Majesty, he is unworthy of your Majesty's notice . . .

King : We will hear the man himself speak. Let him be brought forward.

(*The man is dragged before the king*)

Who are you? Where did you drop from?

Mara : Your Gracious Majesty, I am an unworthy dog. But I have a word to convey to your Gracious ears; and after I have uttered it, I shall gladly allow myself to be trampled under the feet of the mighty elephant which bears your Royal Person.

King : Where were you all the time? On the tree?

Mara : Yes, Your Majesty. I was there since the cock crew this morning. I knew the Royal passage lay here.

King : Waiting on a tree! You could have asked for an audience.

Mara : They stoned me at sight; and commanded me to take myself out of the village; when I still appeared they tied me up and put me in a cellar, but the man who was my jailor, though a giant in appearance, has the soul of a baby. He let me go when he heard of my dream and the command of the Goddess. And I slipped out unseen and climbed this tree, and hid myself in its leaves, waiting and praying for Your Majesty's gracious arrival.

King : What do you want?

Mara : Now listen to me, Most High. Where Your Majesty now stands is a sacred spot. There once stood the great Hanuman on the day Lakshmana was wounded in the battle-field at Lanka and lay in a deadly faint. Guided by omens Hanuman came here, and then went up the mountain in whose shadow Your Majesty is resting now. There on its crest he found *Sanjeevini*. He flew to Lanka with it. and at its breath Yama's messengers fled, and Lakshmana rose to his feet with a new life. Such was the power of *Sanjeevini*; and where it grew there arose a stream, which came down the mountain and now flows past your Majesty's feet. It is called the *Veda*. Its water is the very life-blood of Your Majesty's humble subjects.

King : Does the stream flow on ·all the year round?

Mara : Your Majesty, I am coming to it. The water has flowed on since the day Hanuman took the *Sanjeevini*. Its birth is in the mists of the mountain-top, and it passes through rare flowers and herbs which clothe the mountain-side, before it comes down to our village. And what do we do? My Lord, here I will repeat the command of the Goddess: As I lay in my hut, one day, She stood before me, her tresses flying in the wind; there were stars in her coronet; a ruby as big as the eyes of that elephant, sparkled on her forehead for red mark, her garment was of gold woven with lightning. A look at her, and I knew it was the Mother. I fell at her feet and She said: 'This river *Veda* is my very own plaything. It carries in its bosom the nectar which revives gods and nourishes mortals . . . But when the summer sun bakes your soil, I keep my pet sheltered in the cool glades of the mountain, and then you die of drought. When the sun goes and you have water again, you take what you want but allow the precious stream to dissipate and perish in the foul marshes far off . . . I command you: Tell your king to build a bank and not to let *Veda* leave the village. Give her a home . . .' These were the words of the Goddess: I have repeated them. Your Majesty may trample me down under your elephant now.

King :

Far from it. You have the grace of gods upon you. Your words are weighty. . .

When we return this way tomorrow accompany us to the Capital.

SCENE THREE

Many years later. Mara is standing before his hut on the bank of a vast lake. There is a mingled noise of wavelets breaking upon the shore, cries of gulls, and the rustling of tree leaves.

Mara :	(*Hallooing*) Boy, little man, Ganga, Ganga.
A Distant Voice :	Father, I am coming.
Mara :	Where are you gone, little man?

(*Sound of running feet.*)

Ganga :	Here I am father. You are shouting as if something or the other had happened. I was only behind that tree watching . . .
Mara :	What were you watching?
Ganga :	There is a man fishing in the lake.
Mara :	Fishing. Fishing! Where?

(*Runs. Son follows him.*)

Mara :	Hey, man, get up! What are you doing here?
Man :	Nothing.
Mara :	Nothing! Then why that rod and hook in your hand? And how did all this fish come into your basket? Did they walk in while you were watching the sky? . . .

161

	Go, man, go before you are pushed into the lake.
Man :	No. No. I was not catching fish. I speak the truth.
Mara :	I have been a watchman of this lake for years out of count, and I have come across hundreds of storytellers like you. This is my last warning to you. If I see you again with that rod and hook, I will push you into the water: and the fish will feed on you. Do you understand? Now here go your fish back where they belong. Do you see my son? When I am gone you will be the guard here; this is what you must do with killers, whether they come with arrow for the gulls which skim over the water, or with the hook and rod for the fish. This place is sacred and belongs to the Goddess; and her command is that nothing that flies or swims or walks in these parts should ever be killed. From my hut I have often seen at dead of night a tiger coming down the hill to slake its thirst at that distant corner . . . But even that has to go untouched; such is the command of the Goddess, and the king's. Now begone, you fish-catcher . . .
Man :	You are after all only a watchman. You are not the master of this place. Are you not taking upon yourself more than your duty?

Mara :	I am the master of this place. The king made me so. But for me *Veda* would have run away and disappeared, as she was doing before. I gave her a home, where she stays, and nourishes the fields of thousands of the king's subjects . . . Now look along the bank; do you note its length? A throw from the strongest sling will not take a stone to the other end of the bank; and I, by the king's order, watched every stone with which this bank was built . . . and I open the gates that let the water into the fields. I know how much to give and when to stop, I tend the lake, and see that it is not polluted by man or beast . . . Even that headman of the village who once beat and bullied me, will have to beg my permission if he wants to touch the water. Here I am the king; no one can question me. Now go away, I have spoken to you more than you deserve . . .
	Now little fellow, my son, you see that man there taking his cow to the water's edge. Run on and tell him not to take it there; it is over a coconut-tree deep at that spot. If his cow slips . . . Tell him to move off a little. Go on, go on. (*The boy runs away*)
A Visitor :	Mara.
Mara :	Oh, brother, when did you come?

Visitor :	Just this moment. I left my village at sundown yesterday: and I have walked without a pause.
Mara :	Come into my hut and share my food. There is something you can munch, though not a feast. My wife is away. I and my son are running the home.
Visitor :	I have come all the way to ask a favour of you. You know our village is the farthest in our king's domain; and crops parch up and cattle are dying of drought. Will you give us some water?
Mara :	Certainly, brother. It is here for all the king's subjects to take. Tomorrow I will come with you and see where you can lay the channel, and as soon as it is ready, water will be let through according to the law laid down by the king. Ah, do you notice there the heart of the lake muddying! It was sapphire-like only a moment ago. Ah, see those clouds at the mountain-top . . . there is heavy rain there . . . *Veda* is swelling and carrying mud and flood into the lake. I must keep an eye on her tonight . . . (*calling*) Boy, come away.

SCENE FOUR

Late at night. Torrential downpour and a shrieking storm. The King's Palace. The bell at the palace gate ringing incessantly.

King :	Who is so urgently summoning me at this hour? What has happened in this terrible night of storm? Go down and see who it is.

(The bell ceases, and sound of footsteps.)

	Who are you, man? What has happened that you should be calling us at this hour? Why are you gasping so badly?
Man :	I have been running.
King :	In this storm? Who are you? What has happened?
Man :	I am Mara, watchman of the lake, Most High.
King :	Ah, Mara! How you look battered by this rain, all that water dripping down . . . .
Mara :	I beg Your Majesty's Grace for bringing my presence here in this state. I have come running, battling with roaring wind, and through slush and raging torrents . . . Forgive me, Your Majesty. I am trembling with the message. May I utter it?
King :	Yes.
Mara :	My lord, it is the . . . It is about the lake . . . It is about the lake . . . I feel faint to mention it.
King :	Oh, tell me, is the lake in flood?
Mara :	It is about to smash its bounds . . .

King :	Mara, are you mad? Are you sure your mind is your own?
Mara :	Your Majesty, till the evening there was no sign of a rain. It was a beautiful bright day, unruffled, the lake mirrored the blue sky on its bosom. But at dusk the sky darkened. I called in my son and shut the door of my hut. Rain drops battered my roof. At midnight the wind rocked my hut. I got up and went out. My heart was disturbed.
King :	Oh, tell me, is the lake in flood?
Mara :	I rose from my bed and went out. Ah, I have never seen anything more terrible in my life, my lord. *Veda* was thundering down the mountain; the wind shook the earth. I went to the edge of the water, the waves rose to a man's height and hammered at the bank; the water level was just a hair's breadth below, about to boil over.
King :	Mara, Mara, was the lake . . . ah, what is to happen to all of us?
Mara :	I fell down and prayed. The Goddess stood before me. Her tresses were wild, her eyes gleamed with a strange light; she carried a sword in her hand and she had splashed her forehead with vermilion. I cowered at the sight of her. 'Get up and hear me intently,' she said, 'I am the Goddess of the lake, and that river *Veda* is my plaything. Clear out of

your hut at once.'

'Mother, save me. What is going to happen?' I asked.

'I am going to kick away the miserable stones you have piled up to imprison the waters of my *Veda*. I am going to destroy your tank.'

'Mother, we put it up at your command,' I said.

'Yes, and now I want to destroy it. It is my mood now. *Veda* is my plaything. I created it when I wanted it, and I will splash it away when I like. Who are you to stop me?' she replied.

King : Mara, Mara, are you speaking the truth?

Mara : Your Majesty, may my son and wife perish if there is a word of untruth in what I am saying!

King : Go on with your story.

Mara : I pleaded with her. I pointed out to her the vastness of the lake, the water stretching the length of the hill and going in a bend out of sight; the whole of it kept back by a bank, which would take a quarter of a day to cross . . . But all that she would say to it was, 'Why do you make much of it?' I told her that all that water waited like a crouching tiger and would spring upon the hundred villages and towns and the king's capital beyond, if the bank was removed. She laughed at it and flourished her sword. I pleaded with her for hours to spare us and have pity on us poor mortals. But she was not to be moved. A most terrible and reckless mood of destruction seemed to have come upon the Goddess. I fell on the wet ground, prostrated before her and begged: 'A poor mortal like me cannot stop you, oh, divine mother. But grant me this. I will run to the capital and inform the king, and return. Till then stay your hand. When you see me here again, you may carry out the devastation.'

'Yes, I grant it. I will wait until you have told the king and returned,' she said; and here I am, Your Majesty.

King :	Mara, are you sure you saw and heard all this?
Mara :	How can I prove it, my Lord? Here you see the mud on my clothes: When I fell prostrate before the Goddess, all this mud stuck to me.
King :	I dare not think. I do not know what to do. In a moment or less I and this palace and my subjects . . . All right. Hey, call someone . . . Let it be announced by beat of drums that this is the last day of the world. The deluge is upon us. Tomorrow the sun will rise upon a lifeless land.
Mara :	Your Majesty, permit me to . . .

King :	Tell me, what have you to say?
Mara :	I have a suggestion.
King :	Go on.
Mara :	The Goddess will keep her word. She has promised to wait till she sees me back there. Make it impossible for me to return there, Your Majesty.
King :	How?
Mara :	If Your Majesty's sword is there . . .
King :	No, no. What a horrible suggestion!
Mara :	Or send for the executioner, my Lord. My son is still sleeping in the hut. My last request is this: when I am gone make him the watchman of the lake, and after him his son, and then his son's son to the last generation of our family.

SCENE FIVE

In front of a shrine on the lake. Ganga and his son.

Ganga :	Son! Son! Come here.
Son :	Coming, father.
Ganga :	Where were you all this time?
Son :	I was watching the gulls flying over the lake, father. How they skim and catch fish! It is lovely to watch.
Ganga :	Well, well, didn't you know this was the hour of worship at the shrine?
Son :	Father, I forgot.

Ganga :

Don't forget again, that is all I can say. I will be very angry if you ever miss another worship. You are old enough to realize your duties. I was less than your age when I was ordered to take my father's place. Even my mother was away. The last I saw of my father was when I went to bed. When I woke up in the morning the hut had blown off, and the lake was nearly rolling over the shore. And whom should I see as soon as I woke up but the king! He said my father was no more, and ordered me immediately to do my father's duties. Soon after that he built the shrine, which looks over the lake. And on the day of dedication he was himself present . . . You see those two figures, son. The one on the top pedestal is of the Guardian Goddess of this lake. And the one immediately below is my father, who was known as Mara the Mad. By the king's order, worship is performed on the evenings of every Tuesday and Friday. Scores of devotees come from even distant towns. You must not miss a single worship hereafter.

Son :

Yes, father.

Ganga :

Good boy. When I am gone you must watch over this lake. Now come into the shrine.

(*Ringing of temple bells*)

Appendix 3

THE RESTORED ARM

The following story is based upon the traditional accounts of the life of the famous sculptor, Jakanachari, who built the Belur, Halebid and other Hoysala temples, in the reign of Vishnuvardhana (twelfth century AD). For purposes of the story a few changes in detail have been made.

The temple at Belur was nearly ready. At the next Full Moon it was to be consecrated and opened for worship. The old sculptor, Jakanachari, was working on the main image of the temple in the inner shrine. He spoke to no one and tolerated no interruption. As he was working he noticed a shadow falling on the wall. He had ordered that no one was to be allowed to disturb him. He turned sharply with a curse on his lip, but he swallowed the curse quickly, fell down and touched the floor with his forehead. The king had come in noiselessly.

'You go on with your work,' said the king.

'I obey,' said the sculptor. He was working on the drapery of the image. The king watched the image, fascinated, as godliness grew upon it with each stroke: there was grace in its eyes and protection in its gesture. . .

The king said, 'Jakanacharya, I am longing for the day when I may offer worship to this Kesava. When will you finish your work?'

'Sire, by God's grace, I hope to finish the work by full moon. . .'

When the king left, the old sculptor, plying his delicate chisel, conjured up a vision of the day of consecration. At the auspicious moment while priests chanted and smoke curled up from the sacred fire, he would place the God on his pedestal. He could almost hear now the babble of voices. And the king stood on the threshold of the shrine with the minister beside him, having arrived in state on his elephant; people from all over the empire were crowding in for the occasion. As the image was fixed to its pedestal, a great cry of joy went up from the crowd, and the king presented the sculptor with a gold bracelet. . .

Jakanachari did not break off for food at noon. In the ecstasy of vision he forgot hunger. Someone had the kindness to remind him. He merely replied, 'Get out and don't talk to me.' A little later he turned from the image and was annoyed to see someone standing at the doorway, watching the image.

'Go away,' said the sculptor.

'Yes, I will go away as soon as I have seen as much of the image as I like.'

'Oh, oh! Who may you be?'

'I am a wanderer. I happened to pass this way and dropped in to have a look at the temple.'

'Get away now or I will have you pushed out. No one must see this image before it is completed.'

'I am one interested in stone. I can do a little work myself.'

'Oh, you are a master, are you?'

'I don't say that. But ever since I can remember I have loved stones.'

'You are an upstart. Now let me see nothing more of you,' said the old man.

'Say what you like,' replied the stranger. 'I have gone round and seen all that is to be seen. The pillars are divine; the figures on the outer walls are the work of a godly hand. This temple will be remembered by coming generations as the greatest.'

'I do not need your certificate.'

'Hear me fully,' said the young man. 'I am not speaking now to flatter you. I am merely expressing a fact. I say once again that all that you have done so far is wonderful, except. . .'

Now the old sculptor pricked up his ears and cried, 'Except what? Except what?'

'Except the work you are now doing.'

The old man picked up his mallet and flourished it at the intruder. 'I will smash your skull if you speak any more.'

'At your age you must have greater self-possession,' said the young man. 'I am not saying that your work is bad but your choice of stone is unlucky.'

'Your words are inauspicious,' wailed the old man.

'With that stone you could make a figure for a gateway but not the main God of an inner shrine. After all, the tens and thousands of carvings and decorations are only a setting for the main image, and its stone should have the utmost purity. Now this stone has a flaw, and the image is unfit for worship and consecration.'

'Oh, will no one drag this man away! His words are inauspicious.'

'I am merely warning you with the best of motives. Don't get angry. I repeat that this stone has a flaw, and I am surprised that a man of your experience did not notice it.'

'Young fool, you don't know what you are saying. See this arm: it has chipped and carved fifty thousand forms of

God, but I swear I will cut this off if you prove what you are saying.'

The stranger replied, 'Don't say such serious things. I merely said something about the stone because I thought you might like to hear it. Take it for what it is worth. Don't do such a terrible thing.'

'No, you shall prove it.'

'I will prove it but not if you are going to cut off your arm. I will even say where the flaw is.'

'Where?'

'Around the navel of the image.'

'Young man, I will tell the king and have you put in chains if you don't get out this moment.'

'All right, I will go,' said the young man and turned to go. While crossing the courtyard he turned round and shouted, 'I am going, but bear in mind my warning.' The old man ran after him, gripped his arm, and said, 'Stop now, I will not let you go.' He yelled for everyone in the place. A crowd gathered. He told the crowd : 'This young fool holds that Kesava is made of a stone which has a flaw. If he proves it I will cut off my right arm. If he does not I will cut off his arm and ride him on a donkey.'

The stranger said. 'I refuse to prove anything. Now let me go.' The old sculptor held him by the arm and said, 'Either you prove what you have said or I will chop off your arm and haul you up on a donkey, though if I tell the king he will chop off your head.'

'All right,' said the stranger. 'I accept the challenge. Don't blame me afterwards. Will someone bring me a little paste of sandal-wood?' It was brought. He said, 'May I go near the image?'

'Yes, you may.'

The young man walked into the shrine with the sculptor and the crowd following him. The image stood leaning against a block of stone, looking on all this scene of strife with an unruffled calm. The stranger asked, 'May I touch it?'

'No,' said the old man. 'What do you want to do?'

'I want this sandal paste to be smeared over the image from the chest down. Will you do it?' The old man smeared the sandal paste as directed. 'Now watch it,' said the stranger. The paste dried quickly and stood out in whitish flakes. 'What has it proved?' asked the crowd derisively.

'Has the sandal paste dried all over?' asked the young man.

'Yes.'

'Look at the navel of the image,' said the young man; and where he pointed there was a wet patch the circumference of a little coin.

'It is still wet,' said someone.

'Do you want to watch till it dries up?'

'Yes.'

'Then you may spend the rest of your life watching it, but it won't dry, because underneath it there is a cavity with water, and in that water there may be a toad living.'

The sculptor said grimly, 'I have never allowed anyone to touch my implements but I am about to break that habit now because I may have no more use for them henceforth. Here, take my mallet and chisel and break that navel and show me what is inside.'

The young man was at first reluctant to break the idol, but the sculptor was insistent. The young man held the chisel and with a deft stroke hit out a circular flake at the navel. A little water flowed out, and out peeped a very baffled toad.

The sculptor said, 'My career is now over. I wish I had never been born!'

In that crowd there was a guard with a sword in his belt. The old man snatched it off. 'Now I fulfil my vow, and I gladly do it. I have no use for this arm.' The young stranger wrenched his wrist till he dropped the sword. 'You will not do it. When I came here it was to see all this work and learn whatever there was to be learnt. I did not come here to deprive you of your arm. Now I will be going.' He appealed to those around him: 'Please see that he does no violence to himself.' He added, 'My purpose was only to prevent the consecration and worship of a toad. Please watch this old man . . .' He turned to go. Jakanachari called him and said, 'I admire your feeling for stone. God bless you. Where do you come from?'

'My home is in Kridapura,' said the stranger.

'Kridapura!' repeated the old man and became reflective. 'Kridapura! Who are you? Who is your father?'

'I don't know. I am in search of him,' said the stranger.

'Oh! tell me more about yourself,' said Jakanachari.

The stranger said, 'When I was yet unborn, that is a month before I was born, my father left home one evening and never returned!'

'What was his name?'

'Krishna Deva,' replied the stranger.

The sculptor said, 'Listen now. I will tell you something I know. It was very good of your mother to have sent you out to search for the old absconder, considering the manner in which he had left. But this is to be said for him. He had a life of dedication before him, a life in the service of God. He saw it in a vision. The choice was between family attachments and utter dedication. There was no middle way; and he made his choice abruptly and uncompromisingly, the only way in which any choice in life could be made. And he never looked back with regret because gods above and kings below have been kind.'

'You know so much about him!' said the stranger.

'Yes, because Krishna Deva concealed himself behind a new name: Jakanachari.'

An hour later he said, 'My son, now take me home. My career is over. I may not cut off my arm, but I will never again touch my chisel and mallet. When my eyes and hands cannot discriminate between stone and stone, it is time to put down the chisel and wait for death.'

The sculptor returned to Kridapura. With all the comfort he could derive from regaining home and family he was secretly very unhappy. For he was essentially a creature who throve on his art. And the self-imposed separation from his work was agonizing. He would have withered away and died of this want like a plant kept away from sunlight, but for a dream he had a few months after his return: he was commanded to build a temple in Kridapura and dedicate it to Kesava. He obeyed this command and built the temple, and a number of others along with it. After this the name of the place was changed from Kridapura to Kai Dala, which means: The Restored Arm.

Today Kai Dala is an obscure little village, a few miles off Tumkur. It is known to have been the capital of a state at one time. Nothing of that ancient glory is now left, except the temple with its magnificent Kesava, which stands even today to commemorate the resurrection of an artist.